In These Little Moments

Buddy Lee Walter

Edited by
Nicoletta M. Cosentino

Published in the United States by Open Kimono Publishing, LLC, Thornton, CO

Library of Congress Cataloging-in-Publication Data

Walter, Buddy Lee, author.

In These Little Moments / Buddy Lee Walter. — First edition.

Identifiers:

ISBN 978-1-961763-87-6 (hardcover)

ISBN 978-1-961763-91-3 (paperback)

ISBN 978-1-961763-35-7 (ebook)

Library of Congress Control Number: 2025950215

Library of Congress Control Number available at:

https://lccn.loc.gov/2025950215

Subjects: LCSH—Family life—Fiction. Interpersonal relations—Fiction. Teachers—Fiction. Life change events—Fiction. Creative writing—Fiction.

Classification: DDC 813/.6—dc23 | LCC PS3623.A86 I58 2025

First Edition

Edited by Nicoletta M. Cosentino.

Book design by Open Kimono Publishing, LLC.

Cover design by Juliet Ariel

Cover illustration by Juliet Ariel

First Printed in the United States of America.

Bulk Sales & Permissions

Our books may be purchased in bulk for promotional, educational, or business use. For inquiries, please contact Info@openkimonopress.com.

Follow Open Kimono Publishing

Website: www.openkimonopublishing.com

Facebook: www.facebook.com/openkimonopublishing

X (Twitter): www.x.com/openkimonopub

Instagram: www.instagram.com/openkimonopublishing

For Cate, Juliet, and Alex.

Preface

This is not a "the one that got away" story. Quite the opposite.

The inspiration for this came from a conversation that my wife and I were having with our daughter. An ex-boyfriend was now dating a close friend of hers. Awkward situation. Our daughter and her friend want to spend time together. But there's this ex-boyfriend thing. And, then there's our daughter's fiancé and his feelings about this. Her ex-boyfriend doesn't want to get in the way of the ladies' time together. He also doesn't want to be excluded. Years have passed since our daughter and he dated. This shouldn't be an issue anymore. Or should it? Feelings are feelings. We are entitled to them.

After this conversation, the writer inside my head began playing around with the idea of – what if...? What if someone and their ex's paths crossed again? Would the world end in some sort of cataclysmic catastrophe? Unlikely. Would there nary be a disturbance in the ripples of their lives? Also, unlikely. What would happen?

Prologue

"Between what is said and not meant, and what is meant and not said, most of love is lost."
Khalil Gibran

Chapter 1
AND SO, IT BEGINS...

There is that moment. You are no longer in a deep sleep. You are, however, not yet quite fully awake. The shadow of a delightful dream still lingers. I was with the most beautiful woman.

My head clears a little as I slide into wakefulness. A smile plays across my face with the realization that it was not just a dream. This is my life. And the woman in my dream is lying next to me. The morning light, spilling in through the window, gives her vibrant red hair a stunning glow. I take a few moments to revel in listening to her soft breathing. I fight the temptation to just stay here... simply stay here.

The extrication process, without waking Isa up, is going to prove to be quite a difficult challenge. This will have to be handled with great delicacy and precision. I slip my left hand away from where it was resting around her breast. That is easy enough. But now... now there is the task of moving my right arm from beneath Isa without waking her up.

After some subtle shifting and gentle maneuvering around, I am able to successfully remove my arm from beneath Isa and then myself from the bed. I grab my robe from its hook, slip it on, and slowly open our bedroom door. One last look back at the sleeping Isa and I close our door as quietly as possible.

Once I've made my way from our bedroom to our kitchen, I hesitate as I ponder my choice of coffee mug from the spindle rack. Any one of the Hawaiian ones would go well with the Kona I am about to brew. However, I opt for one of my other favorites. I pour a cup of coffee... just black. I take a moment to scrutinize the subtle patterns of the Kona coffee as it settles into the mug that has my college emblem emblazoned on it. The aroma drifts over the edge of its ceramic container. Next, give the cat her morning portion of food. Luna is already sitting attentively, staring at her food bowl in anticipation. Raise the kitchen blinds and open the window for some fresh air. A delicate mixture of the pleasant sounds of morning birds and the discordant distant traffic drifts in. The scent of the lilac flower bed just outside our window floats through. The simple beauty of the mundane morning ritual.

Stepping out of the kitchen, coffee mug in hand, I move down the hallway and enter the den. My eyes scan the walls of the room. Photos of me and Isa. Photos of our children—well, children no longer children—now impressive young adults. The collection of photos continually being updated as the years accumulate. Our children grow up even more. They spread their lives into new, exciting, and creative areas. More photos are sent to take the place of the photos that have been hanging there. These photos mark the passage of time. They mark the signposts on our children's journeys. These photos mark our son's progress in his career. These photos also mark our daughter's progress in her career, as well as the myriad of different colors her hair has been.

Settling into my office chair, my gaze now rests on the collection of the framed covers of the books that I have written. These book covers have been created by Gen, our artist and graphic designer daughter. They, too, mark the passage of time... from my first foray into writing a book through subsequent endeavors.

I fully embraced my years as a classroom teacher. I loved my encounters with my students. Teaching theatre and English was more of a calling than a job. My students and I all had fantastic experiences working together on productions that I directed at the school. Some of my students joined me when I started my own theatre company and produced shows each summer.

However, the call to be a full-time writer, and the modicum of success of my first few books, was too intense to just ignore anymore. The teacher part of my soul is still being fed enough by my part-time gig as an adjunct teaching the creative writing class at the college. It's a nice place to be at this point in my life.

The coffee mug placed on mug warmer and warmer turned on. A thoughtful gift from Isa. I do tend to forget that the coffee is sitting there when I have delved deep into my thoughts and gotten lost in my writing, only to find it cold when I might remember that it is there.

Time to continue working on the present writing project. First, I get some music going for the right creative work atmosphere. I open my playlists, click, and some 1960s folk music begins.

Each writing project has its own musical background in which I work. Each book has its own rhythm and tone. For my last book I had some British art rock playing. That one had quite a different feel than this one. For this new book, 60s folk is coming along for the ride.

Opening my laptop, clicking on the desired file, then clicking on the "pick up where you left off yesterday" message, I see the unfinished sentence from my last work session. I stare at it. It stares back at me. It's actually more like obnoxiously glaring at me than staring at me. Daring me to finish it. Mocking my hesitation to finish it. The cursor flashing at me in contempt. I make the decision to not give in to that incomplete sentence's harrowing attempt to bully me into completing it.

Time for some productive procrastination to clear my head. Several games of solitaire on the computer ensue.

I check back in on that unfinished sentence. It still has its atrocious attitude about not being completed. It taunts me more. I refuse to give in to its absurd, ludicrous demands. I decide to take a brief sojourn to social media.

After going to my college theatre alumni page on Facebook, I see several requests to join. I recognize two of the names and expediently allow them into the group. The third name is not familiar to me. I check into their personal Facebook page. I see that they did attend the same college as the rest of us and look further to see if they were involved in the theatre stuff. I see that this person is friends with several other members of the group. They are from the older group of theatre people, a little bit before I arrived at the college. It's basically enough information for me to accept their membership request. I allow them into the group and send all three a welcome message.

I had started the group page quite a while ago as a way

to reconnect with some cherished friends from college. Our lives have drifted apart after college. Everyone is scattered around the country. Some might have made it back to campus for an alumni weekend. That was, however, a rarity.

The older group, those that were already at the college when I began, did have their own reunion each year. Although I knew that slightly older group and we had worked together on many productions, I was still not really part of their inner circle. They had bonded with each other before I got there. Still, I do have close friendships with several of them.

This theatre alumni page is an interesting mix of two different sets. There is the older one, those who I had become friends with when I started as a freshman. During my junior year, I seized the opportunity to take a leave of absence and study performance art and pantomime in England as part of a study abroad program. When I returned for my senior year, many of those that I had known were gone. There were different students there now. I had engaged in various relationships and friendships with this new set of theatre people.

When I started the theatre alumni page, people from both the older and younger groups joined. Both of them got to know each other. Some of them bonded with one another. That was kind of groovy... being the lynchpin that brought these people together.

There is an interesting Facebook phenomenon. There are these people for whom I was nothing more than a peripheral acquaintance with at college. We knew each other. We had classes together. We worked on productions together. Nothing more than that. On this alumni page, however, we have connected quite deeply. Now, as adults, we share some common insights and experiences. There are some thoughtful, powerful, and interesting conversations going on with these people.

Then there are those who I considered, at the time, true partners, friends, and companions while at college. Now some of these people barely acknowledge me on the page. A select few do not even acknowledge my existence at all. They are part of this Facebook college alumni group. I can see that they do, indeed, see my posts. They do not post anything. They do not reply to any of my posts. Or to anyone else's. They do not click on a "love" or even a "like." Yet, I can see that they are seeing the posts. They are there. They are like ghostly spectators... silently watching. That's their loss. I don't have any interest in even thinking about whatever issues they may have after all these years with engaging with the rest of us. The rest of us are having a great time reliving some past experiences and sharing new, exciting things happening in our lives now.

Enough procrastination for the moment. There is some writing I should be doing.

However, just as I am about to log out, one particular post catches my attention. There is a comment in there from Laurie... my college ex... on someone else's post.

If you ever want the quintessential example of a messy, problematic, "I have absolutely no interest in ever speaking to you ever again" breakup... well, there it is. Laurie is sharing something about her youngest daughter who just graduated from college. I have never replied to any of her posts or comments. Neither has she ever responded to any of mine. We are both members of this Facebook group. We swirl and circle and dodge around each other without making any direct contact whatsoever. We have never crossed the line. We haven't communicated in—wait, I need to figure out how many... subtract... then carry the... using my fingers might help... nope, still can't... there's a calculator on my phone... where's my... oh, I left it in the bedroom... don't want to risk waking Isa up... wait... the computer has a calculator... I go to the calculator on the computer and work out the math... thirty-six... thirty-six years... since...

I hover my cursor over reply. It would be nice to say congratulations or... something. The group is always sharing the accomplishments of all of our kids. I can't do it. I shouldn't do it. Just can't cross that line.

I hover my cursor over the react icons. I pause at the care icon. Nope. Too much. Definitely not the heart icon. I slide my cursor over the like icon. Nope. Still can't do it. The wow? No. I go for the laughing icon... now I'm just being... oh, just forget it.

I go to write my own comment on the post. Something about congratulating any of our children out there who are graduating and moving on with their lives. I do so. Just as I hit post, I notice another recent post.

There has been this idea of getting together with whoever is available floating around for a while. Sort of a reunion thing. I had suggested it some time ago. Thought it would be fun to have the older group and the younger group get to know each other... other than just posts on our page. Several ideas had been tossed around. I thought it would be cool for us to gather together in Central Park and see a performance of Shakespeare in the Park... go to the Peculiar Pub in the Village afterwards. That idea never worked out. The performance dates at the Delacorte Theatre always seemed to be unworkable with most of our schedules. Dylan, one of the older alumni, has offered his rather large house, which seemed to be a somewhat central location for everyone, as a place for a gathering to happen whenever was workable. Now, it seemed like this was happening in a little while. Several group members had already commented with some sort of variation of "I'm in" or "Not a good weekend for me. So sorry I can't make it."

I respond.

Fairly sure we are in. I do want to check with Isabelle to make completely sure we don't have anything else going on that weekend. Looking forward to seeing those of you I haven't seen in such a very long time and meeting those of you I've never met in person. Should be groovy!

A memory comes out of the depths. One of the older members had mentioned in a post, when he first joined the group, that when he was away from campus doing his student teaching, he did visit one weekend. He shared a memory of coming to see our production of *Cabaret* but ended up hanging out backstage instead. I must have walked right past him backstage and just not thought anything about it at the time. I probably nodded a greeting acknowledgment at him. Just someone whose path I had crossed thirty-some-odd years ago. So, I did—sort of—meet him before. Now we've connected on our alumni page.

While I am having this recollection, a notification of a personal message pops up. I click to see the message. Courtney is, apparently, online and has seen my comment.

Hey, Isaac... did you view all the other comments in that post about the reunion get-together?

No, I didn't see all of them. Yes, I'm procrastinating a little when I should be writing. I read a few of them, but, no, I didn't take the time to scroll through all of the earlier comments.

Thought you might want to be aware... before you make any plans... Laurie is going to be there... with her husband. You okay with that?

Seriously? That was thirty-six years ago. Another time. Another place. Another us. And, aside from a brief descent into shock stupidity, I got over it. Why? Do you think she would have a problem with me being there?

Brief descent into shock stupidity... I like that. It's perfect. Well, you both have the right to be there... it would just be awkward... just saying. Just thought you should know.

I'm fine with it. Yes, awkward because we haven't seen or spoken to each other in over three decades, but... well, there it is. I also haven't spoken to Evan, Freddy, or Maggie in three decades either. Laurie and I can both be in the same place at the same time. I don't even think I have anything to say to her, except hello. I definitely don't see us ever establishing any kind of relationship... I mean, a friendship or anything, but we can be cordial to each other.

Okay. Just thought you should be aware. How is the new book coming along?

Not really sure yet. Got distracted having a Facebook chat with a friend.

Got it. You want to get back to writing.

Not really. No. But thank you for the pleasant distraction. I'm not really feeling the inspiration yet this morning. My brain wants to wander. But that is sometimes when I get my best ideas. I'm just waiting for them to arrive. Are Blake and the kids doing well?

Everyone is well. Blake is coming to the reunion thing with me. If both you and Laurie are there... it'll be an interesting evening. Wouldn't want to miss it.

Why is this still an issue with you after all this time?

The history. The drama. The curiosity about what would happen.

You know I love you, but you're a jerk. When we are all

at the reunion, you are likely to be sadly disappointed at the lack of drama. No one cares anymore. I know I don't. Don't you have anything else to occupy yourself with except me and an ex from my ancient past?

Not really. My life is a vast wasteland. Just kidding around. I'm just having a bit of silliness. I'll let you get back to work. Oh... wait... what's the music this time?

6os folk.

Cool. See you and Isabelle at the reunion!

This conversation is over. I click on the post's comments and scroll back to see that Laurie did, indeed, reply that she would be there with her husband. It looks like twelve or fifteen others have also already replied that they will attend. Enough people to possibly just get lost in the crowd if needed.

I will, of course, get Isa's take on the situation. She has a couple of former boyfriends that she is still in contact with. And then there were those five or six guys Isa was dating when she and I met... or was it seven... no, it was six... maybe it was seven... anyway, that number dwindled down to just me. I am still in contact with several of my former girlfriends... well, at least the ones where the breakup was amicable. And this is not about reestablishing any new contact with Laurie. It's just about Laurie and I being at the same social gathering. Isa and I have a marriage that is secure enough that things like former girlfriends and boyfriends are meaningless. And then there's Gene, one of Isa's former... I guess, "dating partners" might be the best way to describe their relationship. Somewhere in the flow of things he, along with his wife, circled back into Isa's life. And we have a great friendship with them. They will actually be here for dinner with us tonight—part of the group of friends we get together with once a month or so. But... still...

about this reunion and Laurie thing... I really don't want to put any of us in an uncomfortable situation.

I hadn't really thought about Laurie or the breakup in... oh man, I do not want to attempt math again. It has been a long time.

Chapter 2
WELL, THAT DIDN'T WORK OUT LIKE I HAD PLANNED (AKA THE FLASHBACK)

Passion can lead you into some unexpected places. This can sometimes be a pleasant thing. This was not one of those times.

The Trailways bus made a rather tight swing around a curve in the road. I had to shift slightly in my seat to compensate. As I readjust, I let my gaze wander out the window. While still many miles away from my destination, I was in the part of the state that I loved. Especially this time of the year. Late September in this part of the state was just incredible and stunning.

The throbbing of the bus engine melded with the rhythm of some alternative rock music in my earbuds.

It had been quite an arduous trek already. Since I didn't have a car to use at the time, the journey began with a bus ride from the New Jersey side of Staten Island, all the way across Staten Island to the ferry terminal. Then the stench-saturated ferry ride. This was followed by a reek-ridden subway ride uptown to Port Authority. I then had boarded the Trailways bus that would be taking me to where I was ultimately heading.

All of that—the stench, the noise, the crowded bus... ferry... subway... another bus... faded away as my thoughts wrapped themselves around the woman who would be waiting to greet me at my destination. My heart beat a bit faster. It had been a few weeks since Laurie and I last saw each other. Too long of being apart from each other. She had started her senior year and I had started graduate school, but being apart was difficult. It felt like a part of her was missing from me. A part of me was elsewhere.

The song on my music playlist switches to another and I continue to watch the world speed by outside.

Out the grimy bus window were colors that the layers of dirt could not dull. Vibrant golds—vivid reds—flamboyant ambers—sparkling yellows—brilliant oranges. The blur of the foliage whirled past the window.

This was the time of year when Laurie and I first happened. I had seen Laurie around the performing arts building quite often. I was involved with Karina at the time. Even though my relationship with Karina was just a casual thing, my attention to Laurie didn't go much beyond just knowing who she was. But then there was that party at Laurie's house, getting the casts of the two different productions, *Grease* and *She Stoops to Conquer*, together to hang out... glances and stares across a crowded room... lingering behind at the end of the evening as everyone else came to the realization that it was time to leave... at least for them. A whispered, "Those stares have been getting to me all night." Karina and I were no longer a couple after that.

As uncomfortable and long as the ride was, I took solace in losing my thoughts in where I was heading to, who I was going to go see... and the music coming from my earbuds.

This five-and-a-half-hour bus ride finally ends as the bus pulls into the Trailways station on Market Street. I gather my things and step off the bus into the waning daylight. I take a moment or two to stretch a bit. I had been sitting for over five hours, aside from that brief stop in Woodstock when I was able to get off the bus for a few minutes. I inhale deeply. The air has the sharp scent of a crisp autumn evening. The sun is only just beginning its descent, leaving the sky a brilliant, deep azure. I do love being here. I feel as though I became more... me... here. And Laurie is here.

It had been a little while since I was last here. Senior year. Living in the house on Brook Street. That was a lovely, intoxicating time. Almost everyone in the house involved in theatre. Almost everyone in the house involved in the last production I directed while I was here. Morgan, Charlotte, Sophia, and Lana downstairs. Terence, Evan, Laurie, and me upstairs.

After a little bit more of a stretch I begin my walk to Laurie's house by swinging around to Chestnut Street and striding past Water Street. The slip of paper where I had written Laurie's new address, since moving out of the house we shared until I graduated, in my hand, I move forward. I smile as the all-too-familiar sign of the Black Oak Tavern looms ahead on my right. Laurie and I will also have to stop by La Potpourri sometime over this weekend. I am so looking forward to sitting across from Laurie at a small table just for us to share a carafe of wine, hand-holding, and conversation.

As I approach Main Street, stopping for a barrage of traffic, the sign for the Novelty Lounge appears on my right. The sight of a few other familiar bars—it is a college town, after all—greets me.

After crossing Main Street, then Wall Street, and then Church Street, I spot West Street up ahead. Up to this point, I had been focusing on simply being back in the place that has always felt more like home than any other place. My walk had been calm and measured. I notice that, with the building anticipation of who I was about to see, my pace has quickened. I want, ever so much, to just rush there as fast as possible. I fight that impulse. I pause for a moment to collect my thoughts. I check my pocket for everything I need. I check the number of the house on the slip of paper once more. I take in a deep breath and continue on to West Street.

The last song on my playlist ends. I turn off the music and tuck my earbuds away in my backpack. After turning the corner onto West Street, I spot Laurie's house. I stop where I am. I revel in the beauty of this particular moment. I smile. The pre-night sky is glowing gloriously with the very last remnants of the day. A soft breeze gently wraps itself around me. My thoughts wrap themselves around an image of Laurie... perhaps waiting for me in anticipation, as well, on the other side of her door that I see just ahead of me. My heart begins to beat faster again. I take a few more heartbeats to breathe deeply... preparing myself for the next step... for my next few steps up to her house... to knock on her door... to see her again.

A few steps closer. A few steps up to the door. A knock on the door. A doorknob turns. A door swings open. And there she is.

The next few moments are simply a sublime swirl of stepping in through the door... Laurie and I greeting each other... putting my backpack down... Laurie and I ending up sitting on her couch. And then she said it...

Don't be so happy to see me.

What is it?

I think we should see other people.

There is a pause.

Have you met someone else?

Laurie seems to have an involuntary reflex reaction of putting her hand over mine.

Oh, no.

She removes her hand quickly. There is yet another pause.

Do you want me to leave?

No. You can stay the night and leave in the morning.

The next thing I was even remotely aware of was a throbbing noise rising in my head. Can that really be my heart pounding like that? Whatever happened after that moment was lost in a haze of sheer shock.

Chapter 3
AND WHERE THE HELL IS MY SOUL?

The next morning, while in this state of utter bewilderment, Isaac somehow manages to leave Laurie's house. He somehow manages to retrace his steps along the same path he used only a few hours earlier to arrive at Laurie's house. He somehow manages to make it back to the bus station. He somehow manages to board a bus heading back to the city.

He settles into his seat on the bus and absentmindedly stares a vacant stare out of the bus window. Although a few hours ago, when he first arrived, the view was welcoming, pleasant, and beautiful, now the view was... well, not that anymore. Isaac's only other conscious thought at the moment is how his world was completely different a few hours ago.

In the deep recesses of his mind a barrage of questions slammed and tumbled against each other.

What just happened? And why did it happen? And why did it happen now? And why did it happen the way that it did? And when did things change? And when did things go wrong? And where was I when she was deciding all this? And what did I do? And what didn't I do? And what do I do now? And where the hell is my soul? Last time I checked it was there.

These questions go unanswered.

As the bus pulls out of the station to make its way south, he reaches for an object he had carefully stowed in his pocket. As he brings it out of his pocket, as he fumbles with it in his still shaking hand, the morning sunlight streaming through the bus window catches the brilliant cobalt blue of the dolphin ring he had meant to use as a pre-engagement ring.

A tear drops to the ring... and then to the floor of the bus.

Chapter 4
THAT TRANSITION CHAPTER

In my peripheral vision I catch a glimpse of a shapely, exposed leg peeking out from a blue robe in the doorway to the den. Another distraction. But a welcome one. My thoughts leave the past behind.

Good morning, my love.

Good morning, hunny bunny. How's the writing coming along?

Kisses are exchanged.

Not much is happening. I may just try to work on this one for another day or two. Right now, the next step is eluding me... hiding in the shadows. I'd like you to take a look at this transition chapter at some point, to get your thoughts. If I can't figure out where to go with this, I'm just going to put it aside for a little while.

It'll come to you when you stop thinking so much about it. It always does.

This is true. But this time it seems like this one is working in its own time frame. I still have the other novel about the hippie commune to continue writing or the book on Shakespeare's fools to start. There are other projects for me to work on.

I'm going in the shower before getting ready for work. Care to join me?

Nothing more needed to be said.

Chapter 5
A DRAMATIC EXIT

Later that morning, Isa is finishing getting dressed for work. I give her a little bit of help by straightening the collar of her blouse and smoothing out the back of her skirt. Okay, well... the smoothing out the back of her skirt thing... that was more for me than for her... but it elicits a giggle and a kiss from Isa.

After having discussed the reunion gathering, it has been decided that we will go. There is no reason not to attend. Isa's take on it—if the situation doesn't matter to me, there is no reason why it should matter to her. And we don't care how Laurie feels about me being there. I'm not going to allow something that happened over thirty years ago to stop me from seeing other people I care about. I make a mental note to send some money to Dylan as our contribution to the catering for the evening.

We confer on our schedules for today. Isa has several late afternoon appointments at her office. She shows me several of her design sketches to get my reaction. I look them over, comparing them. I point out the ones I like the best.

I was hoping you would choose those. I'm particularly pleased with them.

Isa starts gathering up the items that she needs to take to work with her and getting ready to make her exit. I remind her that I am teaching an early afternoon class and then going to the farmer's market for the last few things I need for tonight's dinner gathering.

What have you decided to cook for this evening?

The almond saffron chicken.

Served in the hollowed-out bread bowl?

Yes.

Great! I will stay out of your kitchen when I get home.

Do.

Akiva will be coming here with me straight from the office.

What about Olivia?

She will meet us here. Is the almond saffron chicken going to be enough for all of us?

Emma and Matthew have tickets to the Caravaggio exhibit for tonight. There will be eight of us this time.

Oh, okay. Is that going to be enough for eight of us?

Sure. I'll just double the recipe.

Recipe? When do you ever use a recipe?

A recipe, my darling, is a starting, jumping-off point... into uncharted territory.

You are, indeed, dangerous in the kitchen. Whose turn is it to bring dessert?

Rick and Gabriel's.

Fantastic! That means some splendid creation from Rick's restaurant! Bye, hunny bunny. See you tonight.

Kisses are exchanged.

Love you.

Love you.

And, with that, she is out the door in a swirl of a skirt, decorative scarf, and a flurry of bags and containers of documents. The door is closed and locked behind her. I turn and begin to make my way back to the den and my writing. I pause as I notice that the room suddenly feels cold and barren without her presence.

Chapter 6
BUT IT'S SIMPLY JUST
ONE WORD

The quiet—or is it silence—of the room is disrupted by my creative writing students beginning to trickle in. First through the door are two young ladies who, although they are deep in an intense conversation, make gestures to greet me... one with a wave of her hand... the other with a smile and a nod of her head. Body language and facial expression tell me that the waver is in the middle of a weighty and troubling thought.

...and then just how long do I wait for him to accept that things are just not working out the way that I need... that I need things to be different before I give up on him and move on?

The smiler, no longer smiling, stops where she is, slightly in front of the waver, and turns to face the waver.

Why are you even with him if you need things to be different? Why are you so invested in this relationship if it's not the relationship you need?

The waver, who has been looking down, looks up at the smiler. A moment of epiphany.

Shit. You are so right. I'm done with him.

The waver takes a moment to fully digest this pivotal moment in her life. A light comes on in her eyes. She glances over at me. There is no awkwardness. We both acknowledge the awareness that I have overheard this exchange. There is no indication of embarrassment or of being apologetic from the waver. Just the acceptance of a truly human, fragile moment in time having just occurred.

The ladies continue their movement toward their seats. The waver's body language becomes suddenly more composed and confident. The weight has been lifted.

This class is broadly defined as a creative writing class. Some students are working on novels. Some are working on screen or stage plays. Some are writing poetry. I differentiate for them when needed. One is working on a nonfiction piece. I differentiate for him when appropriate. This is, strictly speaking, not the right class for him. He is taking it because the nonfiction writing course is not offered at a time that he is able to attend it. He also likes the idea of taking a class with a published author that has somewhat of a reputation. I still, since I have written other types of things as well, help him with his writing. We do accomplish more, however, with our private tutorials than we do with our class time.

Once the class is all settled in, I begin with a few opening thoughts about our writing process.

Wherever you may be in your process or manuscript, brainstorming without editing yourself is imperative. We all second-guess ourselves... question whether an idea of ours has enough, or even any, merit. Fight that impulse. Write everything down. Even if you think it is a useless or even bad idea. Whether you write things by hand or work on a computer, get everything down. And carry around some way to get a note down that comes to you when you are out somewhere. Whether it's notes in your phone or an actual notebook. That thought came from somewhere in your head. And it wanted out. Get it down. Make it real. What you write down is a gateway into your thought process. It can trigger a better idea later. You can change it later. You can cross it out or delete it later. Or it may be that one idea that brings your whole piece together and propels it forward. But, if you don't write it down, you lose that moment of inspiration—creativity—that spark—that came from that place in your brain that you do want to tap into.

Our main focus for today is on the importance of finding just the right word.

We're going to discuss a line from the 2001 movie, *The Lord of the Rings: The Fellowship of the Ring*. At the Council of Elrond, Boromir makes a statement: "One does not just walk into Mordor."

One of my students, who I know is a Tolkien aficionado, and who I was counting on to catch the mistake, raises his hand.

Yes, Ian?

That's not entirely accurate.

Really? Elucidate me.

Boromir says, "One does not simply walk into Mordor."

And what did I say?

You said, "One does not just walk into Mordor."

So, we're talking about the difference between *just* and *simply*?

Yeah.

Does it really make that much of a difference?

Sure, it does.

Why? It's just... or simply... one word.

Because that is what Boromir says. That is the direct

quote. That is what the screenwriter, Philippa Boyens, wrote. But you knew that. I know you knew that.

Thank you, Ian, for helping me make the point. Boromir uses the word *simply*, rather than *just*, because that is exactly the way Boromir speaks. Because that is his voice. "One does not simply walk into Mordor." That is what Boromir would say. Each of your characters has to have an authentic voice. Not your voice. Their own.

I continue.

Which is more effective? The door or our door or my door?

Several responses from the class basically come down to... it depends.

Depends on what?

Another student contributes.

Whether it is a fairly meaningless, just... or simply... a door.

Or?

On whether there is an *our*—a couple or a group—or *my* —an individual—that the door belongs to.

Interesting perspectives. Sometimes it is just... or simply... one word that makes a difference. At this point you can all write a cohesive sentence. Can we make the thought behind that sentence more powerful? Can we make it mean more? Can we make it convey something more about the character's inner thoughts? Their emotions? Their relation-ships? Their backstory? Why did that character choose to use that particular word at that particular time? This, of course, goes for your own voice as the writer, your narrative voice, as well as dialogue from your characters.

I hit the play button on some meditation music for our work session. Sitar music floats around the room. We spend the next forty minutes or so taking a look at their writing projects from this perspective. They are asked to underline, circle, or highlight any words or phrases that could be fidgeted with to entice a little more texture out of. Even the nonfiction piece. Those sentences can still be made sharper with more clarity. We share examples from each student's work and toss around various ideas, helping each find more effective options for some stagnant words or phrases.

After some time spent brainstorming alternative possibilities for their writing, I lower the sitar music slightly and then offer another example of this idea.

What is the response to, I love you?

Several possibilities are provided for our exploration.

I love you back.

I love you more.

I love you too.

I know.

There is, indeed, Han Solo's splendid response to Leia.

Ditto.

Ah, and we have a fan of the movie *Ghost*!

Really? I was thinking this was just a casual thing.

And what about your wife?

Who are you?

Okay, now we're just getting silly. But let's take a little bit of a closer look at those responses... well, some of those responses... to see what subtle things they might be communicating. Love you back? Does that have a slight connotation of—I love you because you love me—that my love for you is a direct reaction to your love for me? Love you more? Does that have a slight connotation of—being a little confrontational—that your love for me is less than my love for you? Love you too? That has always seemed a little awkward to me—like I'm only saying I love you because you're saying you love me. Not that there is anything wrong with that. It is an appropriate response... but, I feel, it is just an okay response. They are all appropriate responses. I want you to think about the subtle things they and other statements might be conveying.

So, what do you say to your wife when she says, "I love you"?

Whoever initiates it, the response is a simple, "Love you." I might add a "my love," and my wife might add a "hunny bunny" to it.

Several of the women and two of the men utter variations of, "aww... how sweet... how cute."

Well, it's a Jessica Rabbit thing.

There is a spattering of giggling to this. Another student adds an observation she has had.

And your wife is a redhead.

This comment produces a quizzical look from me. The student points to the photo of my wife that I have on the bookcase behind me. I nod and continue.

And this is my point. If I were a character in a book—and sometimes I think I am—that is how the character of me would respond. It's still about finding an authentic voice that conveys something more potent and also doesn't convey what you don't want it to. I also, when speaking to my adult children about their mother, don't say, "your mother." I—as me—find that awkward. It feels a little too distant. Not something I want to convey. I refer to her as "my wife." The same as I would if I were speaking about her to you. I also tend to—as me—use the word "speaking" rather than "talking." Think about what words your characters use and don't use.

We again go back to look for words and phrases from which we can tease out a little more fruitfulness. Students take turns reading sections of their projects aloud and we discuss possible alterations.

As the end time of our session looms closer we make it a point to give each student a clear target of something to be worked on before our next session.

Now, I want to leave you with one other thought as we continue to work on your projects. For our next class session, we are going to discuss pivotal moments. It's wonderful to have good, effective character voices. However, also make sure that, every so often, you have a pivotal moment—a moment where nothing will be the same after that moment. You could walk out your door one morning. Instead of turning right, which is what you usually do, you turn left. Perhaps you want to take a more scenic route. Perhaps you want to avoid some obstruction on the right. Perhaps you just feel like it. But in doing so, you see something or someone you wouldn't have, or miss seeing something or someone you would have, otherwise. And that thing you see, or don't see, changes your life. It doesn't always have to be a huge, monumental, world-shattering kind of thing. It, very well, could be. But our lives are also filled with these seemingly little, albeit important, pivotal moments... an occurrence, a comment, a decision, or a revelation, that changes our perspective... that then changes our lives... I mean, your characters' lives. Well, our lives as well.

I look over at the waver. She understands. She ponders that thought. She smiles, gathers up her things, and joins the others as they file out of the classroom door.

Chapter 7
THE ARRIVAL OF THE GUESTS

The scents of fresh marjoram and sage mix with almond and saffron. The kitchen is filled with this aroma as it rises from the oven. Dinner is not quite ready. I join the others in the living room.

We have an intense discussion going on. I lower the volume of the jazz music playing slightly.

Dinner will take just a little longer. Should be ready just in time for when Keli and Gene arrive with the side dishes. What did I miss? What's the topic this time?

Rick and Gabriel were the first couple to arrive with their contribution of dessert. Just as Isa was hoping, it is indeed a splendid creation from Rick's restaurant, which has been stowed in the refrigerator. Olivia, Akiva's wife, arrived right after they did with the hors d'oeuvres and wines, which she has scattered about the room in various locations within convenient reach. She is, at the moment, refilling Rick's wine glass. Isa and Akiva should be getting here shortly. I check the time. They are running a little late. Rick has a question.

Before we get back into our discussion, first, what is it that you are preparing? That bouquet is fantastic.

It's an almond saffron chicken dish. I got the idea from a book about cooking during the Renaissance. But I fidgeted with the recipe a little bit.

I'm getting something more than almond and saffron though. What else is in it?

I'm not one to give away all of my secrets.

You should come and do your thing in the kitchen in my restaurant sometime. A guest-cook kind of thing.

I don't think I would fare well cooking on a larger scale. I enjoy doing it this way... cooking for a small gathering of friends. I know I can have fun and experiment with you. Even you, Rick, even though you manage a restaurant. That can be intimidating. You know, when I was younger, I never would have imagined that cooking like this would be something I would teach myself how to do and enjoy doing. But... well, there it is.

Olivia chimes in as she refills Gabriel's wine glass.

Well that's just great. It's our turn next to host and do the main course. Now I have to follow this? I'm just not as creative as you... in the kitchen, at least. If you know what I mean.

Olivia winks at Gabriel. Gabriel raises an eyebrow. Rick continues.

Cooking is a very creative endeavor. Well, Isaac, the offer is always there. The topic was that... we were discussing our little inner circle here.

Olivia passes me a small plate, hands over a tray of hors d'oeuvres, and pours me a glass of the Malbec. After retrieving the tray and handing me the wine glass, she explains.

Rick was pointing out that none of us work in the financial world...

...or politics...

Gabriel adds...

...or insurance or real estate... etcetera... etcetera...

Olivia picks up her thought...

I'm a violinist. Gabriel is a film editor. Rick runs a restaurant.

Gabriel goes through a list in his head.

Akiva and Isabelle are interior designers. You are a writer and teacher. Keli is an art professor. Gene is the administrator of an arts program. Emma runs a spiritual wellness center. And Matt is a music producer and teacher.

Where are they... Matt and Em... tonight?

Caravaggio exhibit.

Ah. That's nice.

I ponder all this information.

Well, that's how most of us met. Isa works with Akiva. I used to teach at the same school as Matt. I now teach at the same college as Keli. Keli and Isa took art classes together years ago. Isa used to date Gene.

As those words hang in the air, the doorbell rings.

It's unlocked!

There seems to be a little trouble getting the door open. Gabriel is the closest and rises to help. He opens the door to the sight of Keli and Gene, both juggling several containers of food.

Good evening, Keli... Gene... let me help you with those.

Keli calls over to me as they head into the kitchen.

Hi, everyone. Isaac, is it okay to put some things into your oven to warm? Oh, smells great in here.

Sure. The chicken dish is almost done. You can put

your things on another rack. The bread bowls haven't gone in yet.

I turn back to Olivia and Rick.

So, what's the point of all of our interconnections?

Olivia puts together some thoughts.

Well, we didn't necessarily exclude people from those other careers on purpose. We were discussing that our circle of friends here was created, however, because we were all drawn together by the things that were important to us. We just found that interesting.

Rick adds his perspective.

There are actually two different things going on there, though. One is that we were drawn together by our choices of careers—that we all work in very creative areas. Not that you can't be creative in those other areas. But it's really not the same thing. It's more about having an artistic worldview.

And the second thing?

Well, there is the career thing, but there is also the personal connections thing. A few of us work together... or worked together... or took classes together... or we met their spouses through them... or we used to date them.

Right on cue, the trio in the kitchen has finished up their task in there and is joining us in the living room. Gene responds to Rick's comment.

Rick, we never dated... did we?

You would so remember that. And you are so not my type. Even if you weren't straight. We were talking about all our little webs of connections between us.

We were listening from the kitchen. Well, that's how social circles are established.

Keli has come in from behind Gene, along with Gabriel. Each contributes a comment.

People are drawn together by similar interests.

Yes, and this person you know knows that person who introduces you to that person.

Gene's eyebrows converge together as if trying to figure out something.

All of us except Gabriel and Rick. Did anyone ever work with either of them?

Glances go from person to person. A few shakes of a few heads. Keli just silently looks from face to face.

Did anyone ever go to school with either of them?

Glances go from person to person. A few shakes of a few heads. Keli is again silent.

Did anyone ever use to date either of them?

Glances go from person to person. A few shakes of a few heads. Gene scrutinizes both Gabriel and Rick.

So, how exactly do we know you? Did you just wander in off the street and insinuate yourselves into our group?

For the moment everybody present is at a loss for the answer to that question. Some furrowed eyebrows, some heads cocked to the side, some questioning looks from several of us. And then... the sound of the door opening. Isa and Akiva have arrived.

Good evening, everyone. Sorry we're a little bit late. Got detained at the office finishing up a few things.

Welcome home, my love. How do we know Rick and Gabriel?

What?

We were just discussing how we all have all these interconnections between us because of who works with, or worked with, or went to school with, or dated who. How do we know Rick and Gabriel?

Isa and Akiva look at each other and shrug. Akiva seems to be grappling with trying to pull something from his memory.

Wait... didn't Gabriel... no, never mind... that isn't it. Wait... it was at that thing... that time... with that guy...

Keli shakes her head and finally speaks up.

You're all jerks. I was waiting to see how long it would take anyone to remember. Gabriel was a guest speaker at some film classes at the college... which led to us meeting... in the faculty lounge... which led to us chatting and having lunch together... which led to him posing for my life drawing class... which led to Rick hosting a luncheon for that thing... that time... with that guy... at Rick's restaurant... and then the rest of us started going to dinner there often... which led to... well... this.

With that, Keli gestures broadly with her hands out and open, into which Olivia places a small plate of food and a wine glass. Olivia passes a small plate of food to Gene. More glasses of wine are poured and offered.

The sound of the oven timer is heard.

Dinner will be ready shortly. I just need to warm and then fill the bread bowls.

Some move toward the dining table, others into the kitchen, to play their role in preparing for our social circle repast, conversation, and festivities.

Chapter 8
THE CONVERSATION WITH MAGGIE (AKA THE CONFESSIONAL)

After another two days of sparring with this problematic chapter, it is still this vague idea that just refuses to come clearly into focus. The music in the background sets a nice tempo. That's not the problem. It's a deeper issue. Up to this point, my writing has always come fairly easy. Flowing. Almost like... I get this idea in my head... it tumbles around in there... growing... changing... becoming more defined. I let it simmer. If I have created all of the characters and scenarios distinctly enough in my head, it emerges. By the time I start to write it out, it has a life of its own. The characters often tell me where they want to go. Sometimes even surprising me with their choices. This time they are just wandering aimlessly. The plots usually ramble along unconfined. This time it keeps hitting a dead end.

I ponder the thought of skipping over this chapter, moving on, and then coming back to it later. That has worked very well for me in the past. This time it doesn't feel like the correct tactic.

Still, there is a worthwhile concept in there. It's like my

brain, however, is not fully invested in this project. At least, not right now. My brain is also a bit wracked after wrestling with that incomplete sentence. Ultimately, I claimed victory over it and hit backspace until it lost its existence. It felt good... for a brief moment. It ultimately ended up a hollow victory. I now stare at a flashing cursor where that incomplete sentence once was. The muse in my head is being stubbornly silent. Perhaps guiding me to step away from this one. Perhaps guiding me to work on something else. I do not mess with fate when its compass is steering me in a different direction. I've learned to pay attention to that.

So, there I sit, taking a few moments away from my writing to clear my head before making any definitive decision about putting this particular endeavor aside for a little while. I click onto my college theatre alumni page. Yesterday I had posted an image, just adding to the collection of college memories on the page. It was the publicity poster, with the names of the cast on it, for a production of *Just Beyond Reach*, the first stage play I had written. Maggie, a very cherished friend at one point in my life, has left a comment.

Hey, that's my brother on this poster! Which means I probably saw this production too.

I stare at the comment... simply stare at the comment... for a long time... and then I stare at it some more. Although I had started the alumni page, and various members post various things, and people respond to others' posts... this is the very first direct communication between Maggie and me in thirty-six years, since the end of my relationship with Laurie. One might think I was making too much of a minor thing. This, to me, is a life-altering moment. It is a long-sought-after reconnection. A pivotal moment.

I didn't only lose Laurie when our relationship ended. I

had graduated, along with a few other theatre majors. Laurie and most of the others were still there. Things became extremely awkward. I didn't just lose Laurie. I lost an entire group of friends. I lost a huge piece of my life. Losing one relationship was devastating enough. I lost almost everyone in my life at that time.

Jonathan, my closest of college friends, and I visited the college one weekend to see a theatre production of *Last Tango in Huehuetenango*. Laurie was in the cast... something I had not known beforehand and was a bit of a pleasant surprise as I saw her name listed in the program's cast list. I sat there, in the dark of the theatre, watching Laurie perform on stage. It was a strange, alternative-universe kind of weekend. It felt like my presence there was... well, I felt a little like I was being avoided... like I was now an unwelcome outsider. In our estrangement, Laurie had gotten custody of most of our friends.

I wonder what Maggie's reaction will be if I respond to her comment. I wonder if it will be welcomed... or shunned... or ignored. She did, after all, respond to something I posted. Something she had not ever done before. I decide to just go for it. I give Maggie's comment a thumbs up.

Maggie responds quickly.

My brother is not on Facebook, or I would invite him to this group.

I respond back, asking her to say hello to her brother for me.

Do tell him I say hello... we were also in *The Madwoman of Chaillot* together.

She gives my response to her response a thumbs up!

This reconnection, particularly someone in this circle of my college friends, no matter how simple or basic, was incredibly heartening... like finding that one lost puzzle piece to that puzzle that never was finished. Especially with Maggie.

A few moments later, I receive a notification in Messenger. It's from Maggie.

Can we chat?

Of course! It would be great to chat with you!

I have, what might be, a difficult question for you.

Just go for it.

What happened between you and Laurie?

Now, that is a conversation starter.

Are you okay talking about this?

Sure... but if you really want to have that conversation... this is going to be a bit problematic over Messenger. I am going to send you my phone number. Please call me.

Okay.

Several seconds later, my phone does ring.

Hello Maggie!

Hello Isaac. Are you sure you're okay with us speaking like this... about this?

It was quite wonderful to actually hear her voice again.

Seriously? What you're asking about happened over three decades ago. And, by the way, you were the one, not me, that cut off any connection between us.

I was Laurie's friend. It was... strange.

You were my friend as well. I never thought of you as only Laurie's friend. You were, indeed, my friend too. I, of course, would love to chat with you.

What happened between you and Laurie?

Our relationship ended.

I know that.

Our relationship had run its course?

I know that.

Laurie broke up with me?

And I know that.

I just get this feeling that Maggie is trying to find out about more complex things beyond what she has already asked. Things of which she already has a full awareness. Perhaps she is trying to gauge my emotional reaction to this topic. I have no real reason, at this point, to not trust her intentions. I'm also quite interested in seeing where this is going. I decide to play along.

Since those answers don't satisfy you, I sense that you have a deeper, more profound question. Why don't you just go ahead and ask it.

Why did the two of you break up?

We didn't break up. Laurie ended it. As far as the why... I have no idea.

She never told you why?

I can't say.

You can't say... or *you can't say*? ... as they say.

I take a shot at trying to find out what Laurie may have actually told Maggie.

Didn't Laurie tell you why? You were her best friend.

We never spoke much about the why. Just that she felt it was time to move on.

That just doesn't seem quite right. Maggie and Laurie were very close friends. And, as she said, they didn't speak much about the why... but they did speak about it. I decide to let it go.

Well... I must have done something so staggeringly unspeakable that it required the ending of our relationship... so horribly unspeakable that she was never even able to talk to me about it, to tell me what I did... or didn't do— to tell me what was so despicable—so devastatingly unspeakable that the relationship had to end in excruciating silence. And that silence was devastatingly deafening.

Is that the thought that you have been living all these years?

When you don't know... your mind fills in all the blanks. But, no, I haven't been living with that thought all these years. That was just my mind, at the time, going off on an emotional tangent. After a while, my mind created a reason for the breakup that worked for me. That I was comfortable with. That I could live with. That would allow me to move on. I haven't really thought much about all this since it happened.

I hear Maggie inhale.

And what was that? That reason your mind created for the breakup?

My turn to inhale as I prepare my response.

That Laurie and I simply weren't meant to be together for any longer than we were. Laurie just figured that out before I did.

But didn't you want to know what she thought? Didn't you ever want to just ask her why? I mean, so you really knew?

At the time, I was in too much of a state of shock. Afterwards she cut off any communication with me. And I think that getting caught up in that "really needing to know" thing is sometimes a trap. The only point in really knowing why someone breaks up with you is to correct something in your behavior in order to make future relationships work better. Whatever it was in my personality or behavior that caused Laurie to end our relationship self-corrected and led to Isa falling in love with me. Laurie's real reason is a moot point.

I pause while another thought occurs to me.

Well… actually, you know, Laurie might have said something about why.

What do you mean by that?

I went up to visit Laurie that weekend. I walked through her door a man fully in love, preparing to find the opportune moment to ask her to marry me, only to have a few moments of awkward, uncomfortable conversation before being hit with her saying, "I think we should see other people."

What? You were about to propose? Did I hear that right?

It is a little difficult to get a take on if this is truly news to Maggie, or she is feigning surprise. We are, after all, theatre people. I don't have any facial expressions or body language to help me. Just a voice on a phone.

Oh my. I don't know why I thought that you would already know that. I guess it would make sense that you wouldn't. I didn't get the chance to ask Laurie to marry me before she broke up with me. I would suppose that Laurie doesn't even know that. Unless she suspected. Or found out. Or was told. And perhaps that was why she ended things.

I've always had the suspicion that a certain someone, who knew of my proposal plans, made a phone call to let Laurie know of my intentions for that weekend.

I'm still a bit foggy on how it ended.

As am I. Laurie said, "I think we should see other people." I asked her if she had met someone else. She said no. I asked her if she wanted me to leave. She said that I could stay the night and leave in the morning. After that, I suppose, I experienced some sort of shock amnesia. Really, the next thing that I have any clear memory of was walking back up to my house in the city. So, Laurie might have told me why she wanted to see other people. If she did, I did not hear it. Everything after Laurie saying, "You can leave in the morning," is... well, not even a blur. I don't remember anything else until I walked up to my house to find a crowd of people standing there and a neighbor telling me that my brother had just been killed in a motorcycle accident.

I remember that, too.

And thank you, ever so much, for coming down with Laurie to spend a little bit of time with me at the memorial. Although, I have no idea why you showed up.

You called Laurie. Something was said about not knowing who else to call. She asked me to take the ride down with her. Why did you write that letter to me? Was it just to get back at Laurie?

Shock stupidity.

What?

Shock stupidity. It's a phrase I came up with when I was speaking to Courtney.

It does, pretty much, define things well.

I do have a vague memory of sending you a letter. I have no idea why I wrote it or what I wrote in it. Only enough of a fragment of a thought that I knew I needed to apologize to you for involving you in the breakup.

Wait a minute. If Laurie said, "I think we should see other people," what made you think that was really the end of things? Maybe she just wanted to... you know... like she said... see other people... and that included you.

It doesn't make much sense to me that Maggie wouldn't already know the answer to this as well. I also let this go. Perhaps Laurie really didn't discuss the breakup with Maggie in that much detail. Once it was over, this was not a topic of discussion in my life either. It's much more important to me right now to reestablish a relationship with Maggie than deal with some insignificant crap.

When has "I think we should see other people" meant anything other than the relationship is over?

There is a pause.

Never.

And then what? If I agreed to this seeing other people thing? I would be in the city. Laurie would be at college. I would visit as often as I could. She would be seeing other guys. I would not be seeing other women because of how I felt about Laurie. Whenever I would visit, would I be finding things around her house reminding me that some other guy... or guys... had also been there? And whenever we were out somewhere, I would be looking around, wondering which of these other guys she was also seeing. I couldn't live with that while she was just, likely, hoping for me to get tired of the long-distance thing and give up. That was simply just not what I wanted our relationship to be. And I believe I am entitled to my feelings about this.

I pause for a moment in our conversation as I realize my hand has, almost absentmindedly, changed the music that has been playing quietly in the background. My hand switches the music from my Joni Mitchell playlist. My hand has chosen a song from my Bill Withers playlist. "Who Is He (And What Is He to You)?" begins playing.

Of course, you are entitled to your feelings about this. So is Laurie. Did you ever think about all this from her side of it?

Laurie never gave me the chance. We went, in my world, from being in love to this seeing other people idea in one swift moment. If Laurie had said something like, "I'm not completely sure where I want our relationship to go. I'd like to figure that out. I still want you in my life but I think I would like us to really think about what we mean to each other," things would have ended very differently. Unless she really didn't want me in her life anymore. But I wouldn't know that, would I?

So many things get lost in the moment, Isaac, because we often don't know how to react.

That is so very true. I should have tried to step back and do my own figuring out of how I felt about the relationship. That's something I did not do but should have.

I'm not sure what you mean. You must have done that. You were about to ask Laurie to marry you.

I really don't think I did. Or if I did, I didn't think it all the way through completely. This was all so long ago, but I think I was being purely emotional about me being in the city and Laurie being at college. The distance. The separation. Being apart. After being a couple for so long. I don't know. Maybe it was that being more in love with the idea of being in love than actually being in love thing. In retrospect, I think I was just incredibly scared of losing Laurie and maybe I thought that proposing was my only option to hold on to the relationship.

I wait a moment for a response from Maggie. There is none.

If I am really honest with myself, I may have been even more upset about the way Laurie chose to end things, even more so than the actual ending of our relationship. Even a blunt, honest, "I would like you to stay the weekend and for us to enjoy each other's company, but then I need a break from our relationship"—which, of course, would be hurtful —would not have been anywhere nearly as hurtful as a cowardly and disrespectful "I think we should see other people" bullshit line. The scars would not run so deep. And Laurie, obviously, had been thinking about this for a while, and with respect to my feelings and what I thought we meant to each other, the very best she could come up with to end our relationship was a trite, vicious, callous line. That was just so incredibly mean of her. She just wanted to end it and was taking the shortest, quickest, most despicable route.

I wait again for a response from Maggie. There is none.

Ultimately, I have to trust that it all meant something. At least something that deserved more than an ending with a shallow, cruel line. Otherwise everything I believe about love is a lie.

I wait once more for a response from Maggie. There is none.

And Laurie's response to my asking if she wanted me to leave was, "You can stay the night and leave in the morning." She was kind enough to not have me leave that late in the evening—but she did not ask me to stay for the rest of the weekend. She really just wanted me out the next morning. She never said she wasn't breaking up with me. She never said that she wanted to continue some kind of relationship. She never said that our relationship wasn't completely over. And after what I thought our relationship had been—I didn't want to be just another guy she was also seeing. Now, I have to ask why we are having this conversation about this topic now, after all these years.

Okay, here it is. I need your advice. I wanted to ask you how you got through it. My daughter is going through the devastating aftermath of the ending of a relationship. I'm looking for some insights.

Relationships end all the time. You felt the need to end a thirty-six-year silence to ask me about a relationship ending? Not that I mind talking to you. It has been wonderful to hear your voice again—but you didn't know anyone else who had experienced a breakup?

Not a soul-shattering one.

Fair enough.

Not one with no explanation whatsoever.

Fair enough.

Not one that happened totally unexpectedly, without any warning signs.

Definitely, fair enough. But I have to be honest with you... and with myself. There were warning signs. I just did not see them... at the time.

Like what? What kind of warning signs?

Well, things seemed wonderful. I guess they weren't. Laurie and I were spending our summer break at her father's house. Suddenly—very suddenly—at least to me—she says she would like to head back up to college to settle into her new house and get ready for her senior year to begin. That took me completely off guard. But I wanted her to do what she felt she needed to do. I also needed to get ready to start grad school. In hindsight, that was a sign. It simply did not register, at the time, that it was an indication that anything was wrong with our relationship. But she didn't respect me enough to have any conversation at all about why she wanted us to be away from each other—about what was bothering her about our relationship. I simply trusted her, and I accepted her "I need to go get settled in" statement.

Again, I decide to seek out how much Maggie actually knows.

Didn't you ever hear any of this from Laurie?

No. We never went into all of these details.

I guess I should really appreciate that Laurie kept all of this just between the two of us. I thought you, of all people, would know. Being her best friend, and all. Now I feel a bit strange sharing all of this with you.

You never told anyone else before? What about your best friend?

Guys don't really speak to each other that way. I told him that she said we should see other people, so I didn't get the chance to ask her to marry me. So, I guess the relationship is over, and he said, "Bummer. Let's go out and get a drink." So, no… I haven't shared all these details with anyone else. Well, anyone other than my wife. Until now.

Well, like you said, it's been over thirty years. And now I am asking you for some insights about how to help my daughter.

Okay. Well, there was another warning sign thing that I didn't notice at the time.

Like what?

When I went up to visit her at college that weekend, when I walked into her house, while I was standing there being all excited and happy about seeing her again—she was distant and preoccupied. She was probably waiting for her opportune moment for her "I think we should see other people" line. I just didn't see it. I was too wrapped up in waiting for my opportune moment to ask her to marry me.

So, how did you get through something like that and heal?

Trying to get through it is not the right tactic.

What do you mean?

When you try to get through something, your focus is on some vague, obscure idea on the other side—this thing—that you are trying to get to. I had no idea what was waiting for me on the other side. I couldn't grasp on to something that just wasn't there… yet. It felt like I was falling down a deep, dark abyss and frantically trying to grasp onto the walls as I was plummeting down. But the walls are smooth… nothing to grab onto.

So, what did you do?

Instead, I concentrated on what I was doing at that and every specific moment. Lots of people focus on the getting through it part. Getting to the other side. Instead of focusing on some incomprehensible end result, I concentrated on what was happening to me at the moment. I concentrated on the journey through... on what was actually happening to me.

I get that. That makes sense.

There is also this element of trusting that the cosmic tumblers will, indeed, someday fall into place. But only if you listen to where fate is leading you and you don't fight it. It's an issue of—to borrow a phrase—collateral beauty. I will not be trite and say look for the silver lining in this horrible event. However, I do strongly, truly believe that every negative thing that happens to us in our lives does present us with a, often hidden at first, collateral beauty... a positive... something better... if we're paying attention carefully. What happened between Laurie and me simply had to happen in order to put us both on our correct paths. I was not supposed to end up with her. She was not supposed to end up with me. We were both supposed to end up with the people we did end up with. Everybody won.

I suppose that is something good to focus on. How do you feel about Laurie now?

There it is... perhaps... the real question and Maggie's reason for contacting me.

I don't feel anything about her now. I don't know her now. The Isaac I was back then had known the Laurie she was back then. I've been six or seven different Isaacs since then... maybe eight... no, six... perhaps it was seven... no, it was six...

Get on with it.

The Isaac I am now does not know the Laurie she is now.

And the Isaac and Laurie you both were back then don't exist anymore.

Only as a dim memory.

For some of us, that's the only Isaac we know.

Not my problem that some of you are holding on to an antiquated image of me that is long gone. Are you the same person you were in college?

Oh, dear lord, no.

Well, there it is.

But this thing did happen to the Isaac you once were... by the Laurie that she once was.

I can't imagine, nor would I want to imagine, my life without Isabelle or my children. I am so incredibly, thoroughly, overwhelmingly grateful, and thankful that Laurie broke up with me before I asked her to marry me. She stopped me from making the biggest mistake of my life. Wow... that came out kind of nasty. I apologize. I really didn't intend it to be malicious at all.

But I get where that is coming from.

In no way am I trying to be cruel. I'm just trying to make a point. It would have been the biggest mistake of both of our lives. The ending of my relationship with Laurie was the most fantastic, remarkable, transformative event of my entire life. It redefined who I was as a person, who I was as a partner, who I was as a lover, who I would be as a husband, who I would be as a father. Without that happening to me, I would never have become the Isaac that Isabelle fell in love with. Yeah, this part of it takes a huge amount of patience. But the eventual outcome is incredibly worth it. The emotional scars are badges of honor that we should wear proudly. I hope that this would help your daughter.

It could. Thank you for being so open about it with me.

You're welcome. This has just been... strange... thinking about all that again after so many years... It's so very detached now... It's like it didn't even happen to me... like I'm just sharing a story about something that happened to someone else.

Well, like you said... you're not the same person you were back then. So, in a way, it did happen to someone else.

Which is actually quite an amusing point of view to me when I think about it that way.

Are you trying to make a joke?

No.

Because I actually find that quite humorous.

Oh... in that case... yes, I was trying to make a joke.

Amusing thought. Now, both you and your daughter need to understand that none of this will help... not for a while. Did the breakup happen recently?

It did. I mean, not just, but fairly recently. And then, with the reunion happening and with possibly both you and Laurie being... I kind of connected the dots and thought it might be helpful to get some possible insights from you.

If the breakup happened recently, then nothing is going to get through until your daughter is ready. She needs to go through her own grieving process first. Do you know the legend of the phoenix?

I do.

Well, we can all rise from the ashes, transformed, much better than we were. But first... well, you know... there is that damn burning part.

So, what do I do in the meantime? She says she feels like she's lost complete control over everything in her life...

that everything she believed was true about the relationship turned out to be a lie. She says that she just keeps going over things in her head over and over again trying to figure out what went wrong. She's questioning every decision she made about their relationship. She doesn't feel like she wants him back after all this, but she doesn't want to go through anything like this again.

I get that. I felt the same way. Don't push. Let her grieve. Be patient with her. Tell her to be patient with herself. It will take some time. She has lost a part of herself. An extremely important part of herself. She has to regrow that part of herself back. Laurie shattered my soul, but as it healed, it transformed the way I saw myself and the world. Laurie and I were together for about a year... a year of our lives becoming intricately woven together. We weren't just dating. We were living together. We were working on productions together and choreographing dances together. It takes time to unravel lives after that. Unraveling lives is an excruciatingly painful procedure.

I give Maggie a moment to digest that thought before continuing.

Every once in a while, repeat the two parts. One—don't try to deal with getting through it. Deal with what it is doing to you right now, in this moment. Have her ask herself if she is okay with what it is doing to her. There is no right or wrong answer to that question. It is more for self-reflection than it is for answering. I wasn't okay with what my grief over losing Laurie was doing to me. I needed to do some-thing about that. I had a life I needed to get back to. Two—look for the collateral beauty—trust that it is there. Fate is steering her toward something better. But she has to be ready for it and open to it when it presents itself. I met Isabelle by accident. When I wasn't even looking. But I was paying attention to the cosmic forces and to where they were steering me. And... write this down...

Okay.

Are you writing this down?

Sure.

Tell her—Sometimes you just have to be done. Not shattered. Not devastated. Not ravaged. Just done.

That's good. I can tell her that.

Did you write it down?

(Pause) I am now.

Groovy. Something else to write down. Quite a few...

Hold on... not ravaged... just done. Okay. Go ahead.

Quite a few writers have said something like, and I'm paraphrasing here, we are all broken... that's how the light gets in.

I like that. Yes, I'm writing it down.

Like you said she is doing, your daughter will ask herself —a lot—over and over again—like I did at first—why it happened. Tell her not to look for explanations. They will never be good enough. I, of course, would still like to know why Laurie ended our relationship. It's human nature to want some type of closure. But I didn't have to know the reason for the breakup to be able to let it go... move on with my life... leave Laurie behind... because explanations really do not help to heal the soul. Only one person in the relationship needs a reason to end it. However weak or perhaps profound that reason is, that explanation is meaningless in the grand scheme of things. As much as I would love to know why Laurie needed to get out of our relationship, explanations don't change the fact that she just needed me out of her life.

That makes sense.

I hope this all helps. If you think it might be difficult for your daughter to hear any of this from you, her mother, have her text or call me.

Thank you for offering that. She and I have a good, open relationship. I think she will listen to me. Wow. This has all been quite an interesting and profound conversation.

And Maggie?

Yes?

Hello Maggie! It is really, really nice to hear from you. How are you?

I'm well. Oh... I just got a promotion at work.

That's great. Congratulations on the promotion. And how is Jim doing?

My husband's business is flourishing... finally... after a few rough years.

Well, that is great to hear.

I've read your books. They're good. They're very... they're very you.

I'm pleased that you've read the books... and like them. I'm having fun writing them. Most of the time. Just confronting an idea right now, for this new book, that is just not working. I think I need to take a break from it and work on something else for a while.

I gave my daughter a couple of your books to read also. She's a little impressed that I know you... knew you... you know what I mean. Maybe I will have you call her. She would get a kick out of talking to the author of books that she likes.

Do. I'm hip to that happening. But have her call me. Let her decide when she wants to do it. Put her in the power position. It will help her to have control over something specific.

I sense that this is the opportune time to change the

subject and mention something I've been meaning to discuss.

I noticed, on the alumni group page, that you said that you are going to be at the reunion thing. At Dylan's house.

Wouldn't miss it.

There is a pause. I hear Maggie inhale. She continues.

You do know Laurie is going to be there.

I can't help wondering if this bit of information is also a small element of Maggie contacting me... trying to gauge how I feel about this.

Yes, I do.

You good?

I am, indeed, very good.

It really will be nice to see you again after all these years.

I'm looking forward to it.

We spent the rest of the phone call reminiscing and rekindling an old friendship. That was very nice to finally be able to do.

Chapter 9
SO...WE MEET AGAIN

It really is a glorious summer night. A stunning sunset is in the rearview. The drive to the reunion is quite a pleasant one. Only a touch of heavy traffic for a moment or two. Isa and I find a spot to park at the end of the street and exit the car. The scent of food being prepared in the Mediterranean restaurant we passed a block over drifts by us. A breeze gently darts in and out around us, playfully amusing itself with the edge of Isa's dress. I take her hand and we head down the street. Along the way we chat about those she is about to meet.

Isa already knows Jonathan very well. As my closest college friend, we have tried to see Jonathan and his wife as much as we can. Isa and I reminisce about a fantastic time, when the kids were young, meeting at the college for an afternoon of Frisbee, the kids rolling down the hills, and a wonderful stroll around campus.

We've had coffee or drinks with Courtney and her husband, Jim, every so often. Then there was that trip to Albany to see Vincent at the café he runs.

Isa has met Morgan once. We ran into her at an alumni

weekend thing. The others are only known to Isa from the stories I have told her and the photos I have shown her. Some of the former Brook Street housemates will be there. Some of those I've been in productions with will be there. And there are those that will be at the gathering that graduated before I started college, or after I left, that I only know from the group page and have never met in person.

As we arrive at Dylan's house, the sounds of various voices, laughter, and music flow out from inside. The semi-transparent curtains on the windows present us with a shadow play of activities going on beyond them.

A few steps closer. A few steps up to the door. A knock on the door. A doorknob turns. A door swings open. And there she is.

In the open doorway stands Laurie. This catches me off guard. I was preparing myself for this moment, although I just did not expect to encounter Laurie so soon. Like... right at the door, before we even entered the house. Like... Cerberus guarding the gates of the underworld, perhaps? Cerberus' job, though, is to prevent the dead from leaving... not the living from entering... at least not without permission from Hades. And I am fairly sure Laurie is not a hellhound. And I am fairly sure she doesn't have three heads. I look at her. She doesn't have three heads.

Hello.

Hello.

Our eyes meet. Pause. Deep breath.

May we come in?

Well, now... that depends.

Depends on what?

On who you are.

Oh, you don't remember me. I'm not sure if I should be insulted or relieved.

Just attempting a little bit of humor to deal with an awkward moment.

I understand. I get that.

How did I do with that? Okay?

Yeah... fine.

Dylan just asked me... us... to get the door because I... we... were standing near. I... we... didn't know it would be... This wasn't...

It's okay. Really... it's okay.

An exchange of uncomfortable, perhaps nervous, smiles. Laurie's face is the same. A bit older, as we all are, but still the woman from my memory. Laurie's eyes flit from me to Isa standing slightly behind and to my right, and then back to me. Laurie breaks eye contact with me and looks down. As she looks back up, her hair falls over her face. She brushes it back from her face with her hand and tucks it behind her ear. Laurie inhales as she starts to say something... it seems like she is changing her mind and stops... there is a thought rattling around in her head... and then it seems like she decides to just go for it...

I don't know what we are supposed to do here. Do we simply nod at each other? Do we shake hands? I would venture to say that a hug is not a good choice.

Laurie casts a glance back at this guy standing behind her, just inside the house.

So... may we come in? Let's start with that.

Oh. Yes. Sorry.

I take Isa by the hand and attempt to move through the doorway. Laurie has not yet stepped aside.

It is okay to come in, isn't it?

Yes. Sorry. Like I said, awkward moment. I'm just a bit...

Yeah... me too.

Laurie moves aside to allow Isa and me to step through the doorway. A little cluster of guests forms nearby after we have entered, and the door is shut behind us. Me... Isa... Laurie... and this guy that I do not know that I presume is Laurie's husband. I become aware of a variety of little collections of the college group in the room. A few are trying, ever so very hard, to appear to be still in the midst of their various conversations. Their eyes, however, are on us. Not all of them. I would think that whatever happened between Laurie and me hardly even registered with most of them. Perhaps just a vague awareness—Laurie and Isaac are a couple—and then—Laurie and Isaac are no longer a couple. That was the extent of the situation to them. To me —a pivotal moment in my life. To them—something hardly worth taking notice of. Life is like that.

We stand there, unsure of what the next move is. Still, there is an air of calm that I had not anticipated.

This is my wife, Isa... Isabelle. Isa, this... this is Laurie.

The women assess each other. I resist the urge to smile at this. For some strange, bizarre reason, I am enjoying this moment... ever so slightly... perhaps it's the uncertainty of the situation... I suppose it's the writer in me... the question of how this is going to play out... of how I would write the encounter. Isa speaks up first.

Whatever you may think, it is actually nice to finally meet you.

Which is, actually, the exact line I would have written. It's gracious and nonconfrontational, but not too overly warm or welcoming. And the *finally* adds a bit of abstruseness to it.

Thank you. That is gracious of you. It's nice to meet the woman Isaac ended up with. This is Paul, my husband.

Paul and I assess each other. We give each other a

perfunctory nod. First impression—he seems like a decent guy. He has kind eyes. But not the type of man I would have thought Laurie would end up with. I would have thought she would have been attracted to a hipper, edgier, little more "a little bit dangerous" kind of guy. Especially since I was not the kind of man she wanted to end up with.

Handshakes are eventually, tentatively, exchanged. As I touch Laurie's hand—our first physical contact in over three decades—I look into her eyes. A mixture of questioning... uncertainty perhaps... bewilderment... and a touch of bemusement. I think I'm feeling the same.

Silence ensues. I break the silence.

Isa and I are going to go say hello to the others. We'll chat later... perhaps?

Laurie and I look at each other. There is, at the moment, no indication of how this is going to go... if we will, indeed, chat later... or if this will be the extent of our speaking to one another.

I'd like that.

Isa and I begin to move off to join another group over in the middle of the living room. I overhear a comment from Paul and Laurie's response.

You okay?

Pause. Deep breath.

Yeah... fine.

Isa overhears this as well.

How about you? You okay?

Pause. Deep breath.

I'm good. I want to introduce you to some people. I want them to meet you.

Far out. Let's do this.

Isa and I first head over to where Jonathan is. We interrupt the conversation going on with the priority of a big hug.

Jonathan always gives the best hugs. Hugs that embody a deep friendship. Hugs that, just when you think they might be over, hang on for that little bit longer. Hugs that make the time apart slip away. We chat for just a little bit and catch up. Since we have seen each other fairly recently and we want to reconnect with those we haven't, we let him get back to the conversation he was having, excuse ourselves, and say we will be back later.

The next hour and seventeen minutes swirl by with conversations with Maggie, Courtney, and others. The twelve to fifteen I first thought would be here is more like twenty-five to thirty, scattered about the house in small bunches. I neglected to factor in the significant others. Some people have claimed their territory, particularly near the drinks and food. Some are congregating with those they were in college with—some close friend groups. Others seem excited by the prospect of cavorting from bunch to bunch—getting to meet those they had not known before, except via the group page.

Isa and I grab drinks from the dining room table. More guests arrive. There are hugs, handshakes, and introductions to the significant others I have never met. A couple of our couples met in college and married. That's really cool—charming and sweet. There were a few college couples that I definitely thought would survive into marriage. Not all did.

Some of us have remained very close and see each other whenever possible. Some of us have not seen each other since college. Photos of our children on our phones are being passed around. Some of our children have followed our paths into theatre, music, or other arts. Also, really cool. Carrying on the tradition. Everyone is enjoying sharing the highlights of our lives. Although all of us are connected with each other on the group page, most of that information tends to be relegated to memories from college and big new events in our lives now. Not all of us are connected on our personal pages where we share these other parts of our lives.

Looking around the room I also notice the absence of Evan, one of the Brook Street housemates. I lost contact with him after graduation. After getting on Facebook, and again when I started the alumni group page, I searched for him. Came up with nothing. I ask around. No one has had any contact with, or even knows what happened to, Evan.

More drinks are passed around. We congratulate and toast to each other's endeavors and successes.

We also, sadly, toast to a few of us who are no longer with us. David is among those who have died too early. I have very fond memories of him. My first production at college was *Cabaret*. David was a senior and playing the character of the MC. He was a senior and I was a freshman, but he was very friendly and welcoming to me. There were a few others, mainly some juniors and seniors—I take a look around the room and spot several of them—who felt it beneath them to associate with a lowly freshman. David was not like that. Although we only had the one year together, we spent quite a bit of time around each other.

Several of the others have read my books or, at least, a book or two. Maggie adds that they are an enjoyable read. I thank her for the kind comment and add that I did think of myself as a writer just creating some enjoyable reading, so I appreciate her opinion. As other information is being passed around, I learn that Laurie has recorded an album of her music and is working on a second one. I am honestly happy for her. Music was her passion. Seems like it still is.

Most of us were theatre majors. There are several of us, although not theatre majors, who were very involved in the theatre productions so are still members of the group. A small group of us followed the theatre path and are working actors, directors, or tech people. Another small group went on to pursue advanced degrees in theatre and are teaching in colleges. One of us, a music major, even returned to teach at our college as a lecturer in the music department. There she is, right over there with the musical theatre bunch. Still others had their life paths take them to places other than theatre but are involved in their local community theatres. It is an eclectic gathering.

Many of the older group are retired. Some of them are living out what I referred to as their "second acts" as I am with my writing. They are pursuing their passions as artists or musicians or returning to theatre after a career of doing something else.

Everyone is getting a kick out of meeting Isa. She is a vivacious presence in the room and fits in well with my college friends. A crowd of theatre people can be a tough audience. Isa, although not a theatre major, was involved in her college's theatre productions, so that helps. Not one of us, but still one of us... if you know what I mean.

Throughout all of this, as Isa and I travel from group to group chatting with everyone, Laurie and Paul occasionally appear on the outskirts of various small gatherings, adding to the conversations. Nothing is brought up about our past. Every so often, as Laurie is chatting with some group elsewhere in the room, I think I see a few glances in my direction. But I might, very well, be reading into that too much. At a serendipitous moment I slide past Courtney, lean in close, and whisper, "See? No drama." Courtney smiles and nods approvingly at this... but still mutters a sarcastic, "Damn, too bad."

An hour and seventeen minutes into the festivities this thing happens.

Isa and I are chatting with another small group. In this cluster is Amelia, one of the alumni that I was only familiar with because we worked on a production together. I wouldn't describe her as a friend. Just an acquaintance. She introduces us to her husband, Derek. In the midst of various conversations, I find out that Derek is a fairly high-profile publicity consultant. He mentions several of the publicity campaigns for which he has been responsible. I'm familiar with a few of them and am a little impressed. He's good at what he does and has a very creative, slightly unconventional, daring, "jump right in," avant-garde approach to things that I appreciate. The conversation turns to another topic and Derek's occupation is forgotten about for the moment.

Laurie and Paul join our group and become part of the conversation. Amelia congratulates Laurie on the success of her album. Amelia says she likes Laurie's music. The question of if there is a second album happening is asked. Laurie's response is that she is working on a second album. Then the question of when this new album will be released is asked. Laurie says that she is not quite sure about that. The first album was the better songs from her live performances. She says that there are other songs that are exciting when performed live with an audience right in front of her, but don't really work very well on a recording. So, right now, she is kind of stuck until she can write some better material for this second album. Laurie admits that she is dealing with a little bit of writer's block, and nothing is being written just yet. She says she needs more songs for a full, complete second album. Laurie adds that she has some music written for a few new pieces, but she's stuck on writing lyrics for them. Laurie says that she does have a few other songs she could use. She's just not thrilled with them. She says they're a little too trite and she wants some higher quality songs for her second album. She also admits that the record label she is working with is not too happy about that. It seems they want to capitalize on the success of the first album and release a second one fairly quickly, but she wants to deliver some stronger material for this one. Derek, who up to this point hasn't really been paying that much attention to the conversation, has a sudden realization.

Wait a minute. You're that Laurie? I've heard your music when Amelia was listening to it! Nice stuff.

Laurie thanks Derek for the compliment. I decide to add to the conversation.

It's difficult, when you're writing, when the idea that you need to move forward is being elusive. I'm actually at a point, with the book I'm working on—was working on— where I'm not sure where I want to go with it. I've stopped working on that one... put it aside... at least for a little while.

Now Derek is paying full attention to this conversation. Derek has another sudden realization.

Wait a minute. You're that Isaac? The writer?

Yes.

I'm sorry. I haven't read any of your books. But I know who you are... I mean, your reputation... I mean, about your books.

Derek's two realizations combine to become an epiphany.

Oh, this is too good of an opportunity to pass up.

Amelia looks at her husband.

What's too good to pass up?

Her music... his words... together... good! I can make great things happen for you both with that! Here's my card.

There's a stunned, *what did he just say?*, moment as Derek reaches into his coat pocket, extracts a couple of business cards, and hands one to Laurie and one to me. Isa and Paul share a moment as they look at each other. Paul raises an eyebrow. Isa shrugs. Derek continues.

Isaac just said that he's taking a break from writing the book he's been working on. Laurie just said that she's having trouble writing lyrics for a few more songs. What's the downside here?

Courtney deftly enters the conversation.

This is not such a good idea. Laurie and Isaac were once...

I make eye contact with Courtney and shake my head. I see, in my peripheral vision, Laurie also shaking her head. Courtney gets the message that neither one of us would rather this topic be brought up. Courtney stops mid-sentence. Derek looks confused. I'm sure he thought the reaction to his idea would be... well... something different than this.

What? What is it?

I look over at Laurie. She looks at me as if searching for an answer to a different question that hasn't actually been asked... at least aloud... yet. She smiles—laughs a little—rolls her eyes.

Oh, just go ahead and say it. It's fine. We're fine. We're fine, aren't we?

There is that question that hadn't been asked aloud until now.

I'm fine. You fine?

I'm fine. We're fine.

Well then... fine.

Fine.

I smile back at Laurie and turn to Courtney.

Courtney... just go ahead and finish what you were going to say.

Are the two of you okay?

We said we were.

Okay. I was just going to say that Laurie and Isaac used to be a couple.

Derek looks at Laurie. Derek looks at me.

So?

Chapter 10
SO?

Derek's utterance of, "So?" has put everything into perspective. It was actually never that much of a big deal in the first place. It was just the pretense of something that was simply not there. For me, it was an attempt to make sure no one was uncomfortable, and we didn't bring any of our personal issues in to spoil this evening. Turns out, there were really no issues anymore. If there were, they dissipated over three decades ago. Scars have healed. Now it just seems like much ado about nothing.

Derek has offered his publicity services, at his usual fee, of course, which would be a discussion between him and the record label.

You two are doing some interesting things separately. If we get you collaborating, we can parlay that into some great publicity for you both. It'll help the sales of your books, Isaac, if you're also seen as a lyricist with your words on a music album. And we'll attract the audience that listens to Laurie's music. Laurie, you'll be able to finish your second album faster, with contributions from a novelist. And we'll attract the audience that reads Isaac's books. The fact that you two used to be a couple just adds to the mystique of the whole thing. That makes this even more exciting. And fun. And profitable. Trust me on this.

Exciting he says. Maybe. Fun he says. I don't know about that.

Others around us have chimed in with their encouragement. There are a few comments.

Well, aside from that breakup thing, you both did work well together...

Laurie did work with you when you directed that script you wrote, *Life/Show*...

You did choreograph those dances together with the dance company...

Of course, as usual, Courtney has a snide remark.

Some people just want to watch the world burn. I'm sorry. Just kidding. Go for it.

Several ideas are tossed around. Several people ask if we are okay with this. It's getting a little annoying. It almost feels like they're insinuating that we shouldn't be okay with this. Or, at least, they're surprised that we are okay with this.

Although I have a vague recollection of some of Laurie's songs from when we were together, I have no idea what her music is like now. I say so. Laurie suggests I listen to her album. I counter with the suggestion that she read one of my books.

Any one in particular?

Not in particular.

Courtney suggests Laurie start with *Bring Your Own Pencil!*—my first book.

I cautiously agree to dig out some of my poetry pieces to send to Laurie. She cautiously agrees to look at them to see if they fit her style. The atmosphere around our little gathering becomes a little bit lighthearted. Paul turns to Isa.

Just checking. How do you feel about this?

I trust my husband implicitly. You trust your wife?

With all my heart. Not a problem.

Paul reaches out with his hand to Isa to offer a handshake of agreement. As she takes his hand, Isa leans in and whispers something to Paul, which elicits a broad smile and a slight laugh from him. I figure I will ask her what she said to him some other time.

Courtney steps in closer to me.

I know I've been joking around a bit about you and Laurie...

Joking implies that something was funny.

Wow. Yeah, I know I sometimes have a very sarcastic, caustic sense of humor...

And bitchy. Don't forget bitchy.

Anyway. This whole thing is nice. A full circle kind of thing. A cathartic, healing thing. Putting the cosmic forces back into alignment. I'll keep my mouth shut from now on. At least, about this.

A good lesson for us all.

Derek, for whom this is simply a business transaction, asks a question which, I am sure, he does not perceive as the very delicate question it is.

Isaac, are there any pieces... some poems... that you wrote about Laurie?

I hesitate. I look at Laurie. She looks at me and raises her eyebrows almost imperceptibly.

There are some poems.

This just keeps getting better and better. I would think that there would be some great material for the album in those.

Interesting.

74

Chapter 11
A MOMENT AGO

A moment ago, I never thought you would say goodbye.
I walked into this room, a moment ago, believing we were
both still in love.
When did you know we weren't?
Your last words spoken, a moment ago, still echo in my
head.
How long have you been rehearsing them?
Shadows of the people we were, a moment ago,
swirl around the room.
The dark came into the room, a moment ago, from the little
window
above your mirror—
meandering around the edge of the frayed and fading
curtain.
Our lives intertwined, a moment ago, now they are
unraveling.
I try to grasp onto some tattered strand but it's all just
slipping away.
I could hear your heartbeat, a moment ago. Now I can
only hear

my own heart pounding.
My world, a moment ago, made sense.
I held you in my arms, a moment ago, as I have many times
before,
only this time it doesn't feel the same.
Now it's just your arms but it's not you.
The once warmth from your side of the bed
is now thin ice cracking.
I waited, a moment ago, for the sun but hope it won't show.
Shards of sunlight arrived, a moment ago, far too early—
slithering through the window shade to tell me this night is
over.
The love I lost... I swear it was here... a moment ago.

Chapter 12
BURIED TREASURE

Ever since the reunion a few days ago, I have been meaning to get to the task of pulling out these pieces of poetry that I had put in deep storage—both literally and figuratively.

Like a buried treasure—buried—covered over—forgotten about—map destroyed—they are, once again, uncovered.

Not all of them are about Laurie. The better ones are. Perhaps a combination of feeling more deeply at the time, or I simply became a more eloquent writer as time went on.

After Laurie, I stopped writing poems. Actually, I stopped writing anything. The creative part of me was gone. Or, at least, the part of me that cared about creating anything was gone. Although I did have three relationships after Laurie and before meeting Isa... or was it four... no, it was three... those were more or less not very serious things. At that point, I wasn't interested in a serious thing. When I had healed—there Isa was. When my life with Isa began, I vowed to not write any poetry. Every relationship I had in the past that resulted in the creation of poems... ended. I refused to tempt fate. There was too much at stake.

The poet in me, however, had difficulty keeping quiet. I did eventually—three decades later—write two poems for Isa. The first one was a fun experiment with beat poetry, titled "dig"—as in, *I dig you.* The other, *It Was You*, was a far better expression of our inextricable bond to each other.

Sorting through these old poems, it feels as though I am staring at shards of my broken soul that I had left behind... the other one... before I grew back that part of me. I momentarily have a pang of wondering if having agreed to this was the right thing to do. Perhaps these should just remain buried. That moment passes with the realization that none of these scattered words on these pages have any meaning for me anymore. It was just a brief tug from the past that was a meaningless whisper of a previous life. It quickly dissipates.

I do have to figure out which ones to scan to send to Laurie. Any computer files of these have long since been deleted. All I have are these paper copies. These have been in a box with other remnants of the past. In the garage. Up in the loft. In back. Deep behind the boxes of our children's old clothes that Isa can't bear to part with.

Which poems? What to do? Do I send her only the ones about her? They are better. She's never seen any of the poems I wrote about her after the breakup. How will she react? Do I care how she will react? To be honest, not really. But, at the same time, I don't want to piss her off. Laurie can choose to use them, or she can choose to not use them.

There are those poems that I wrote for her when we were together. Then there are those poems I wrote about her after the breakup.

Chapter 13
SHE SINGS FOR ME

Through the haze of my night, I feel your eyes
Two stars dancing in the eternity of my mind
Melting away the chill that lies inside.
Songbird, reach for me... now,
Songbird, sing for me... forever.
Can't believe I can see
All the things you let me see,
Can't believe I can hear
Your sweet whispering in my arms.
Songbird, fly with me... tonight,
Songbird, dance with me... forever.
The beat of your heart as you breathe softly next to me
Warms me more than any fire ever could,
Rising... falling... feeding... releasing...
Again, and again,
As the steady pounding of the wings of the songbird,
Come to carry me home.
Songbird, take from me... always,
Songbird, live from me... forever.

Chapter 14
THE ONE SHE CAN'T HAVE

As I look over the poem *She Sings for Me*, I see that I had scribbled the words *Bird of Prey* on the bottom of the page. I had, most definitely, forgotten about that. Must have done that right after the breakup. Just an emotional reaction at the time, I guess. Perhaps I meant it as a different title for the poem. I don't remember. Somewhere in here, in this collection, there is another poem where I also used the songbird idea. That one would actually be better suited for a transition into song lyrics. It was one of the few pieces for which I wrote lines that could be used as a chorus. That could be one that Laurie might be able to use.

I did get Laurie's album as she suggested. Been meaning to listen to it. Just haven't yet.

As I sort through all of these old poems, I do find the other one where I used the songbird imagery. I put it aside with the others I might send.

Really, *It Was You*, the poem I wrote recently for Isa, is far better than these others. Laurie, however, is not getting that one.

Chapter 15
BEAUTIFUL STORM

If you think of me
When you think of me
Do I bring a smile?

Or did you forget about me?
Do you remember why we fell in love?
Did you ever cry me out of you?

Beautiful storm
Beautiful mistake
Somewhere songbird
Sometime songbird

If you think of me
When you think of me
I hope I bring a smile

Look me in the eyes
Tell me you want out of this and
I'll just be someone you used to know

Buddy Lee Walter

Beautiful storm
Beautiful mistake
Somewhere songbird
Sometime songbird

For you
The perfect ending
For you

You planned everything so carefully
You rehearsed everything so carefully
For you

Beautiful storm
Beautiful mistake
Somewhere songbird
Sometime songbird

When it happened
You had already moved on
For you it was all over

When it happened
It was all just happening to me
In that moment

Beautiful storm
Beautiful mistake
Somewhere else siren
Sometime else siren

Chapter 16
I'VE BEEN MEANING TO ASK...

Do I send these to Laurie and tell her that they are about her? It would probably be better to give them to her without that information. Let her figure it out for herself. Or wait until she asks. If she cares enough to.

There are actually several I may send over that are not about her. There were other women in my life, before Laurie, that inspired some poetry. Pieces still interesting enough for her to work with.

Are you writing? I don't want to disturb you if you are.

Isa's voice comes drifting in from the hallway. She appears in the den doorway a moment later.

No. Sorting through the poems I had in storage. Trying to decide which to send over.

Send them all over and let her decide.

There are a lot here. And some of them are not my best work. And some of them would probably not work as song lyrics without a lot of rewriting. Some of them are pleasingly profound. Some of them are just random thoughts that I felt I needed to get out of my head.

I'm okay with you and Laurie doing this thing. I'm just not getting involved with helping you choose poems that you wrote for other women.

Wouldn't ask that of you. And she's not getting *It Was You.*

Thank you. That one's not for her. What are you listening to?

Just some R&B music to set the mood.

Have you listened to Laurie's album?

Not yet.

That will probably help you figure out which poems she might be able to use.

That is, likely, my next step. Right now, I'm just going to continue to pull out the pieces I think are the better ones.

I will leave you to it then.

Did you need something? Is that why you came in?

No. Just wanted to check in on you, hunny bunny.

Thank you, my love.

Isa grabs my desk chair and spins it so I'm facing her. After leaning over to kiss me, she spins me back to face my desk and turns to exit the room and continue down the hallway.

Wait. I've been meaning to ask. At the reunion you whispered something to Paul.

Paul?

Laurie's husband. What did you say that made him laugh?

I said, "This should be interesting." Is it interesting yet?

I'll let you know as soon as I do.

Isa smiles at this, blows a kiss my way, and goes on about her business. I get back to mine.

Chapter 17
TU ME MANQUES

Glances and stares across a crowded room
Lingering behind at the end of the evening
The swirl of your peasant dress
A mid-afternoon warm breeze drifting in
Through our open window
Sweet sweat dripping
A guitar being strummed softly
Sounds just the same
As I remember

Your voice once felt
A memory in the shape of your mouth
A last kiss
Our second-to-last last goodbye

The side effects of you
Keep it sacred
Keep it precious
Keep it secret
Keep it safe

Buddy Lee Walter

The other side of tonight
The other side of this moment
Morning will be here soon
Too soon

The first day of knowing
That you don't love me anymore
I still have to figure out how to let you go
I feel myself fumbling forward and stumbling back

The crisp days of autumn have just begun
Everything else is ending

When we say goodbye in the morning
You will feel relief
What should I feel?
Hurt for me losing you
Or happy for you
That you got what you wanted?

You did what you had to do
I can only do what I can
Perhaps I was a warm breeze
But you wanted a storm
Perhaps I was a gentle stream
But you wanted a raging sea
Perhaps I am presuming too much
Perhaps I have overstayed my welcome
One less soul here for you to deal with
Mine is gone

Hold me please
But not the way you hold me now

In These Little Moments

With a lie
In your cold, cold arms

Dare I ask you
One last time
To hold me the way you held me before
When I know you can't?

I wake up and my world is all wrong
I just thought there would be more time

Chapter 18
IT'S JUST A DAMN STROGANOFF

Now, promise me you won't compare my dinner to your Renaissance chicken thing...

The almond saffron chicken...

Yeah... that thing... but I could use any advice you might offer.

Olivia is needlessly fidgeting with the beef stroganoff with dill she's been preparing. The others are all sitting about in the living room. I've been lured into the kitchen under the false pretense to be enlisted to help out carrying something.

Everything here looks fine. You go into the living room and do what you do best...

And what is it that I do best?

You host. You pour wine. Refill glasses. Pass around the hors d'oeuvres. Make sure everyone has what they want. There's one thing you can't do.

What's that?

The cook is not allowed to complain or offer apologies about their cooking. We have always all taken turns making the dinner. Why is this such an issue for you this time?

I'm just trying to do something different. I always make the same few things. I wanted to try making something I haven't before... so I did.

We're all friends here. It doesn't matter. Now go. I'll tend to the stroganoff.

The others look up as Olivia sweeps back into the living room. Isa checks to see where I am.

Where's Isaac?

Oh, you know Isaac. He just can't resist kibitzing in the kitchen. I told him I had everything under control and to get out of my kitchen. But, well, you know Isaac.

Isa and Olivia exchange knowing looks and smiles. Olivia does as she was told and swings around the room refilling wine glasses and offering items from the appetizer trays. She calls to me in the kitchen.

Isaac, shall I pour you the Malbec or the Merlot this time?

I'm about to request the Merlot when Ric speaks up.

Give him the Cabernet I brought.

Ric also calls out to me in the kitchen.

Isaac, you need to try this Cabernet.

The Cabernet it is then, Olivia.

I'll bring it in to you.

No need. Everything is going well in here. Things just need to finish simmering a little more. I'll be out in a few moments.

Olivia sets a wine glass for me on the dining room table and moves on to tend to the others.

I exit the kitchen and join the others. I make eye contact with Olivia. She points to the glass of Cabernet on the dining room table, which I then pick up. She then unobtrusively gestures me over to her. As I come up beside her she turns away from the group and leans in. We chat like two spies discussing a secret mission.

Anything else I should do?

You'll just want to add the dill weed when the sauce has thickened just a little more.

I take a moment to enjoy the bouquet of the wine in my glass.

Why not now?

Fresh spices and herbs should be added near the end of cooking.

I take a sip of the wine.

Why?

Do you want to get into this now or finish your dinner? Go check on the side dishes and check the stroganoff in another five or ten minutes.

Olivia looks at me with a slight look of panic in her eyes.

Well, is it five or ten?

Make it seven minutes.

Right. Off I go.

I am about to remind Olivia I said seven minutes but decide to just let her go do her thing. And she scampers over to the kitchen. Emma and Matt, the couple who missed our last gathering, have just finished telling the others about the Caravaggio exhibit. Matt looks over at me.

Isaac, I hear that you are venturing into the music world.

My gaze shifts over to my lovely wife. She smiles at me.

Just thought it would be nice to have the view of someone who produces music.

How much has she told you?

I got the basic idea. This is not uncommon. If a singer is having problems finishing songs, other writers are brought in, so the album gets finished. That is, if it's a new artist. An established artist would just get more time. The record company would have to wait. Studio time is expensive. Studio musicians just waiting around to get to work is expensive. Does she use studio musicians, or does she have a band?

I never thought to ask.

Doesn't really matter. The record company wants what they want, and they have their own time frame for what they want. So, how involved are you?

Not very. I've just sent her some of my old poems to possibly work with as lyrics.

Poems about her?

Well... mostly...

Another sip of the wine.

...yes.

This should be interesting.

Isa's eyes brighten. She sits up and adds a comment.

That's exactly what I said.

I sent her some poems that I wrote a very long time ago and that I haven't even looked at or thought about in a... well, since I wrote them.

Rick chooses this moment to add his point of view.

But she's your ex and the poems are about her. That complicates things.

You say she's my ex as if she was my wife and we've divorced. She's just an ex-girlfriend.

There's no such thing as just an ex-girlfriend.

Now it's Gabriel's turn for a pithy remark.

She's an ex-girlfriend you were going to ask to marry you.

Another sip of wine. I cast a glance over in Isa's direction.

You seem to know all about the situation. I just think it

would be an interesting career move to have my writing in some songs on a music album. Derek, this publicity guy, thinks so as well.

Gabriel leans forward in his chair and directs his attention to Isa.

What's Isabelle's take on this? Isaac reconnecting, granted sort of peripherally, with a former girlfriend?

I am nothing like Laurie. Very, very different. It isn't like Isaac replaced Laurie with someone just like her because he wanted to get back something he lost.

I raise my glass and react to that last statement.

A valid point, my love. Thank you. I had to seriously confront the kind of person I wanted... needed... as a life partner. I came to realize that someone like Laurie was not it. Someone like this...

I gesture at Isa.

...was what I really craved.

Isa smiles, leans back in her chair, crosses her legs, and responds.

Craved. Craved is a good word choice. I like craved.

Anyway, I just gave the poems to Laurie to possibly work with. The rest is up to her. She may not even like them. It's just some poems.

Keli turns her attention to her husband, Gene, who has been suspiciously quiet during this entire conversation. She playfully hits his arm.

Why have you never written a poem for me?

When have I ever written anything? And I definitely have never written anything for any damn ex-girlfriend.

He quickly realizes what he just said and who else is in the room to hear it.

Sorry. No offense, Isabelle.

None taken.

At this moment the Earl Klugh CD that has been playing finishes. There is one of those awkward silences. Akiva saves the moment by adding his thought.

Well, Isaac, do let us know how this music album thing works out.

I will. And Ric?

Yes?

Nice Cabernet.

Isn't it, though?

Olivia calls out from the kitchen.

Dinner is almost ready. Another ten minutes or so. It's just a damn stroganoff. Don't get too excited.

I call back into the kitchen.

What did I tell you?

What did you tell me?

What you couldn't do.

Shit. Sorry. It's a lovely stroganoff.

Akiva, again, shifts everyone's attention.

Come on. Guys, let's finish setting the table. Isa? Keli? Would you help with bringing the side dishes in from the kitchen? Emma, would you mind choosing another CD for our dinner music? Something from the jazz collection.

And with that, everything is in motion.

Chapter 19
AY, THERE'S THE RUB

My background-writing-mood music is one of the only two sounds in the otherwise quiet room. The other sound is the ever-so-faint sound of my fingers tapping away at my laptop keyboard. Inspiration has grabbed me by the throat and dragged me back to my writing.

Ever since I put that last writing project aside, due to what seems like a stalemate, ideas for another one of my novels have been forming more clearly. I often work on more than one book at a time. One is usually my primary focus. The other one—or sometimes other ones—slowly gain existence. When there is enough substance in my head, I like to let it start leaking out of there and onto the page.

I've had this idea tumbling around in my head for quite a while. *Aquarian Equinox* is turning into this story of a commune—a group trying to keep their hippie ideals in the modern world. It's actually coming out a bit funnier than I intended. There are, however, some wonderful touching moments as well. But it works. My head is in a good place for this one.

A third sound is heard. The front door opens and closes. Isa is back home from work.

There have been two interesting phone calls for me today. The one that I answered right away was from Amelia's husband, Derek, the publicity guy. If Laurie does decide to use my poems as lyrics, he would like to have a book of my poems published to coincide with the release of Laurie's album. The thought of publishing my poems, other than the three or four... maybe it was five... no, it was four... that were published in anthologies years ago... is something I had never really considered before. After Laurie I never really thought about my poetry again. That is, until I wrote those poems for Isa. I liked the idea of publishing those since they were definitely not going to be used for the album. Interesting thought. I tell Derek that I would be fully behind this idea as long as it wasn't just the poems being used for Laurie's album.

And then there is what sounds like things being placed on the dining room table.

The other phone call, which I let go to voicemail since I didn't recognize the number, was from Devon, Laurie's album producer and recording engineer. He left the message that Laurie might be interested in using some of what I sent her, but they would like to meet with me to discuss some possible changes to some wording. I don't know how I feel about that. Not the changing of some wording part. That I don't care about. Unless it completely changes the meaning of the poem. I'm not sure about the going to the studio to meet with them part. My encounter with Laurie at the reunion left us unscathed. Don't know if I want to mess with that. Sometimes it's best to leave things as they are.

And now the sound of the foyer closet opening and then, after a moment, closing.

When I returned the call and spoke with Devon, I first asked him to send me notes on what changes they needed and would make them and send them back. Devon said that he understands about my previous relationship with Laurie... and my reluctance to actually come to the studio to work on the changes there... and that was why the request came from him and not Laurie... but they need me to be listening to the music while we were doing this... phenomenally easier to do this in person.

He also says that Laurie feels like she doesn't want to change anything in the poems without me being completely okay with it and she needs me to be the one to make any alterations to them. Devon says this probably might only take just a few days. I tell him I will get back to him about this.

Isa comes around the corner.

Dinner smells good. What is it? What's cooking, darlin'?

Isa leans over my computer and kisses me. She then looks down at the computer.

What's this?

Aquarian Equinox. The story about the commune.

I like the idea of that one.

Isa takes notice of the soft jazz music playing.

Good choice of music to work on this one. I don't recall you listening to this recently... actually, for quite a while.

It just seemed to be an inspiring choice. It sets a nice mood for me to write.

It seems like it would.

I change the subject.

I got a phone call from Laurie's album producer. They

would like me to come to the studio for a few work sessions. She might want to use some of my poems, but they want me there to be the one to make any needed changes to them. Would you mind if I went to the studio?

Why would I mind?

I would be working with Laurie.

Isa takes a moment to consider this.

You're already working with her.

This is different. It's more than just sending them my writing over to them to work with.

It's no different. You are who you are now. She is who she is now. Your relationship with her is not what it was. It is what it is now. Whatever that is.

Okay.

Is this stirring up feelings from the past?

Feelings? No. Some memories, yes. The memories connected to the poems. But not any feelings.

Good memories? Or bad memories?

Now I take a moment to consider this.

Neither really. Just occasional flashes of images... but there's no emotional stuff attached to them.

You do what you need to do. I just don't want to see any of this causing you any pain.

The moment it does, I'm out.

I know that.

Oh, and the publicity guy has an idea about having a book of my poems published. That is, if they do end up using some of my poems as song lyrics. I told him I might be interested in that if it was more of my poems than just those used for the album. They might only want to use a few poems for the album, anyway.

That is an interesting thought. And what about what's cooking for dinner?

I need to go check on that, that's what.

Quickly saving the file I've been working on, I close the music and my laptop, rise from my desk chair, and head towards the kitchen. Isa puts her arm through mine as we walk together. We have to shift positions a little for us both to fit through the door like this.

And what is it that you need to check on?

We chat, arm in arm, as we make our way towards our kitchen.

You did ask that when you came in, didn't you? There's a carrot and shrimp salad with a sesame vinaigrette and I'm making braised beef with a sherry-parsley sauce.

Splendid. Which wine with that? I'll go set it on the table for you.

We'll have the Bordeaux with dinner.

D'accord, mon amour.

Tish, you spoke French! Cara mia!

Chapter 20
SO, WE MEET AGAIN... AGAIN

So, what's the issue you're having?

Devon, Laurie, and I sit around a table in a small workroom area in the recording studio. Through a large window, to the left, I can see two other people working at a sound console. I can hear muted bits of discussion. On the other side of this console, through another large window, there is a space with various instruments and microphones scattered about. There are, what seems like, miles of cables strewn everywhere. Audio speakers are also almost everywhere. To the right is a door leading to a break room—small table, a few chairs, refrigerator, microwave, a coffee maker—the usual.

Copies of my poems are laid out in some piles on the workroom table at which we are sitting. As I look across the table, I can see a few handwritten notes on these. Several words and phrases are circled. Other pieces are underlined. I see quite a few exclamation marks. There are a few question marks as well. Someone has, apparently, been reading these over very diligently and with a great deal of consideration and reactions.

Also on the table are three cups of coffee that had been brought in for us by a sixth person who is presently fumbling around in the break room. Perhaps it's just because I am used to my own specialty Kona coffee—I don't think of myself as a coffee snob—but this coffee is nasty. Not stale. It tastes more like no one has bothered to clean out or descale the coffee maker in a long time. I politely take a small sip of it every so often.

Well, first...

Laurie tentatively begins speaking. Up to this point, all of the conversation has come from Devon—Hi, Isaac—Nice to meet you—Let me show you around the studio—Here's the control room—There's where the singers and musicians do their thing—There's a break room over there—Hey, Bob, would you mind bringing some coffee into the workroom for us?—You want a cup of coffee, right?—How do you take it? Just black. Just black, Bob. Thanks for doing that—This is this—That is that—Let's go into the workroom here and we can sit and talk.

Laurie has said nothing until just now. She pauses and absentmindedly shuffles a few of my poems around on the table. She has not made eye contact with me at all. Devon's gaze shifts from me to her and back. Laurie's mouth opens but no words emerge. Devon is about to say something. Laurie stops him with a glance and she starts. She speaks slowly and carefully.

I... like... these.

I'm pleased you like them.

I wonder why I said that. I could have just said fine or okay. I mean, I don't really care whether or not Laurie likes them. I do care that other people appreciate my poetry. I do care that Laurie likes my poetry enough to use as song lyrics. So, I guess I did mean what I just said. I suppose I don't care if the Laurie—the woman from my past—likes them. But I do care that this Laurie—this songwriter who is sitting across the table from me right now—likes them.

They're lovely. But...

Ah... there it is... the "but."

...I'm not quite comfortable with *Tu Me Manques*.

Why not quite comfortable?

There is another pause from Laurie. Her furrowed brow—corners of her mouth twitching slightly—not looking directly at me—tell me she is struggling with how to say something.

Laurie...

She looks directly at me for the first time since I arrived at the studio. Body language, facial expressions, and tone of voice communicate one thing. Something deeper is going on behind her eyes.

...these poems do not hold any meaning for me anymore. I have no emotional attachment to them. I am pleased if you have an interest in using them for your songs. But if you don't like something, let's change it. You will not offend me.

Laurie looks at me more intently than she has before. She exhales ever so slightly as the shadow of some thought disappears.

This...

She slides my poem *Tu Me Manques* away from the others, across the table towards me.

...is about someone in love with a woman. If I sing it, it becomes a lesbian thing. Not that I have a problem with the lesbian thing. My own daughter is... I just don't feel comfortable going there myself. It would feel false.

I turn the sheet of paper around so that I can look at

what I wrote. I see a particular line circled and a question mark next to it. After a moment or two I offer a change.

What if we take out the peasant dress line?

I like the peasant dress line. I like the imagery. I'm sorry.

Suddenly, a ghost of the past grabs me. And I know I am taking it completely out of context, but hearing the words, *I'm sorry* from Laurie jolts me. Maybe it was the change— the faint tremor—in her voice and the quick movement of her hand—from clenched to open, as if she was letting something go or offering something—when she said it. Maybe I'm just imagining things. Maybe it's just wishful thinking.

I take another look at the poem. I grab a pen from nearby and make a very small alteration. I slide the poem back across the table to Laurie.

Instead of "the swirl of your peasant dress," the line is now "the swirl of my peasant dress" because it's your dress...

Laurie, quite abruptly, shifts her gaze from the poem back up to me.

...I mean, it's the narrator's dress and you're the one singing the song.

She looks back down at the words on the page. It looks to me like she is reading the poem and hearing a melody in her head. Her head bobs slightly up and down to some music unheard by me.

Okay. This works much better for me. Thank you. The rest of the poem is fine. I already have some music in mind for it.

I glance at Laurie and then at Devon.

That was simple enough. That can't be the only reason you've asked me to come here.

Laurie gathers up the bunch of poems on the table.

There are some of these that work very well as they are for lyrics. I just want to suggest a little change here and there. I just didn't want to make any of these changes without you. I mean, I want you to be the one to make any changes.

Fine.

And there are others that I like pieces of. I thought, maybe, we could put together some songs with a part of this one and a section of that one.

Okay.

And, I know you would say it sounds constructed and fabricated... but I like having a chorus in the songs. Some of these have lines that would work as chorus with a little bit of fidgeting.

My thoughts do tend to come out as poetry. Not song lyrics. I don't consciously write a chorus.

That's what I do.

Show me an example.

Okay. Like this one here...

Laurie shifts through the papers for a bit and finds the one she is looking for.

...these lines here. If we repeat them and then add...

We sit at that table working on the lyrics for quite a while. Devon, somewhere during all this, unnoticed by us, had left the room.

Chapter 21
HIGH PRAISE, INDEED

Hey!

Looking up from my work, I find my daughter standing in the doorway to my den. Her vivid pink hair arranged in yet another funky, fashionable way that I have not seen before. The hair color goes well with my violet graduate school T-shirt that she wears, which I gave her since it no longer fit me.

Gen!? Lovely to see you, my dear! How long have you been standing there?

Genevieve comes all the way into the room and around my desk. As she ends up behind my chair, she drops her arms around me and kisses the top of my head.

Just a few seconds. I needed to drop off a few things for Mom. They're on the dining room table. What 'cha working on?

First taking a moment to lower the volume on the song playing from my 70s rock playlist, I gesture to my computer screen.

Two things at the same time, actually.

You do that all the time. I've known you to be working sometimes on three things or more at the same time.

That I do. This is a little different for me. Sit down and have a chat with your father.

She swings around the other side of the desk to drop into the only other chair in the room. She throws one leg over one arm of the chair. She flips her colorful scarf out of the way and rests her chin on her hand on the other arm of the chair.

This is my book about the hippie commune.

Groovy. And you're also putting together a collection of your poems for a book?

Yes. There's that too. So, I guess I'm working on three projects. I'm also working on altering some bits and pieces of my poems to use as song lyrics.

Oh, right. How's that going?

Going well. I'm learning more and more about constructing lyrics. Though I'm not really the one doing it. I'm just making changes that I'm asked to... changes that Laurie is suggesting.

Genevieve swings back and forth in the swivel chair for a moment or two.

And how is that going for you? Working with an ex-girlfriend?

It's really not a big deal.

It really is kind of a big deal. This is someone who, in a different world, could have been your wife and my mother.

A very different world. If the universe had altered its path so much that Laurie and I had married, you would not be the you that you are. And you are far too precious to me.

That's very sweet, Dad. But, you still haven't answered the question. How is it going working with Laurie?

I slowly construct the best, most accurate response to this.

Interestingly. We had one session yesterday. Worked for two hours or so in the studio together. Just business. Just about making my poems work as song lyrics for her. No personal discussions at this point.

Oh? Really?

I'm not sure if we're avoiding the topic or if the opportune moment just didn't present itself or if, perhaps, there is really nothing to discuss.

Are you avoiding it?

You know that I sometimes don't know what I think until I write about it.

Genevieve swings her leg off of the arm of the chair, sits up, and then leans forward.

Seriously, Dad? Just answer the damn question.

After taking a moment to reflect on this, I respond with what I think is the closest to the truth that my conscious mind is going to get.

There were a few awkward... no, not awkward... tense... no, not tense... pensive... no, not pensive...

Stop being such a writer and get on with it.

Okay. There were a few uncomfortable... no, not uncomfortable...

Dad!

Okay. Okay. Strange. There were a few strange moments at first between us. But mostly, it was just about the poems. I think we were both simply trying really hard to establish a pleasant... no, cohesive... no, a...

Dad! Now you're just messing with me.

...a conducive working relationship without bringing in our personal baggage to interfere. We are dealing with some poems that I wrote about us... about her. So, I am sure this will be a topic of discussion when we are ready to go there. Being in the recording studio was kind of fascinating though.

Genevieve leans back in the chair again and swivels back and forth.

That sounds cool. I'd love to see what goes on in a recording studio.

And, I suppose, seeing this woman we've been speaking about has nothing to do with it.

I didn't say that. I am curious, though. About seeing a recording studio too.

Let's see how things go and I'll ask if you can visit. Let's see how long I'm there for. I'm really only supposed to be there, doing this, for a few days.

According to who?

I consider this.

I'm not sure. I think it was the album producer saying I should only have to be there for a few days. It would have to be him. He's the only one I've spoken to other than Laurie.

As you always say, everything takes...

And we both finish this thought together.

...longer than you think it will.

And Genevieve finishes her own thought.

Just be prepared for what may happen. Things may take longer than just a few days.

I change the subject.

Have you spoken to your brother?

Genevieve checks her phone.

I sent Sam a text two days ago. He hasn't responded yet. We had a brief phone chat last week.

Samuel is quite busy these days. The new screenplay is taking up a lot of his time. We'll have to set up a time for a group chat.

I change the subject again.

Now, tell me about what's going on with you. Are you healing?

Genevieve shifts in the chair.

I suppose.

Are you dating anyone?

There is this one woman from my yoga class that I'm kind of interested in. We've become kind of friendly with each other. Asking about each other's day. Things like that. I can't tell if she is interested in me yet. Or even if she's interested in women. I'm waiting to see how things unfold. Not rushing into it. I know it's been a while since the breakup... but no... not right now. I've been spending more time with some friends. I'm not really looking to get into another relationship. I'm fine with it being just me for a while.

Now it's my turn to lean forward.

You just told me to be prepared. You should be prepared as well. That's when I met my wife... when I wasn't looking... when I was fine with it being just me.

That's different. Your marriage is the Olympian ideal for all other marriages that the rest of us can only aspire to. It lives on a completely separate plane of existence. Very few of us other mere mortals get to experience something like that.

Olympus is not the best example of a good marriage. Zeus was definitely not the ideal husband, by any means. Hera had her issues with him. Nor was Hades. Although Persephone did, eventually, grow to love him. And then there's Poseidon and Amphitrite. Now, there's a complicated relationship. But the gods do play by rules of their own.

I hated mythology. I just like saying the word *Olympian*. But you know what I mean.

I sense that this is the opportune time for some fatherly advice.

Our head and our heart engage in a constant quest to be filled. We don't always make the best choices in our zeal to fill the empty spaces. That's part of being human and learning from our mistakes. Make the effort to let go of the harmful crap and give space to the worthy stuff. That's when the cosmic tumblers will place certain people in your life path. Just be open to that moment and be attentive to it when it happens.

Gen just stares at me while various thoughts merge in her head. While she thinks, I add another comment to this.

There will come a time, even though your ex may still be somewhere in the depths of your memory, the thought of them will no longer have any impact on you.

I pause a moment and check to see if Gen is ready to verbalize what she is thinking. I guess not yet. I give her one more thing to ponder.

Many years ago, whenever I would reflect back to my younger self, I would feel a bit sorry for that younger me and the things he went through. I eventually embraced the idea that I deserved... more... the love I wanted... the partner I wanted... the life I wanted. Don't wait too long to grasp that for your own life.

It now seems like whatever idea was in Gen's head is ready to come out.

You know, Dad... you're a Libra... you're left-handed... and you're a middle child. That's like three strikes. You should be such a complete and total mess. But, somehow, you've ended up pretty centered.

That's high praise, indeed, coming from my daughter. Thank you, my little love.

Genevieve rises from the chair and leans over my laptop to kiss my cheek.

That's my cue. Gotta go. Bye, Dad. Love you.

Love you.

As she exits the room, I add...

Call my wife.

And I hear a faint response from down the hallway.

I will.

She probably won't. I make a mental note to remind her of that again.

I decide to rotate my attention to my three projects and work a little on preparing my poems for being published as a book. When I wrote *It Was You* for Isa, I had only handwritten it. She preferred it in my own handwriting. It was time to type it up.

Chapter 22
IT WAS YOU

I look up and into you
Get lost in your beauty and fall deep into your soul
Lost yet found at the same time
On my way to somewhere I didn't know I was going

I see you... just a glimpse out of the corner of my eye
I see you... in a dream
I see you when I wasn't looking
I wake to find you are no dream
I wake to find you in my arms

The feel of you on my fingertips still lingers
The fragrance of your skin still intoxicates me
I see your eyes, staring into my own
I hear your soft breathing
I taste your lips on mine

I've tasted sweet, enticing women
But none like you
My love for you is forever

Buddy Lee Walter

But I fall in love with you again each day

You keep me coming back
I give of myself to you
When you take me, you take all I have to give
Yours for the asking
To take, to hold, to cherish

I am for you as you are for me

Chapter 23
OH, SO CLOSE

Instrumental music spills out from the monitor. Laurie sits on one side of the workroom table. I have found a spot on the floor—I'm a floor sitter—where I can lean against the wall and have a selection of my poems set up in a neat semi-circle around me and a legal pad on my lap.

We've been at this for about an hour and a half or so. Over the last few days, we've managed to work on three songs to the point that Laurie and Devon say they can do whatever they need to do to get them ready for recording. Stuff about arrangements... bass parts... drum parts... background vocals... getting musicians... and things like that. I stay out of those discussions. I'd only be in the way.

I know a little bit about music theory... very little. I know what makes a song work musically. I actually have two bass guitars, an acoustic guitar, a piano, a keyboard, and a ukulele around the house. Used to have a drum kit, too. I play... a little... very little. It's more like I improvise a few things on the instruments. I'm not very good. I can play the notes. I can't play music.

Okay. So, there's the "only a few days" that Devon first mentioned. Yeah. It's now turning into a few more than that. I can hear the echo of Gen's voice warning me of this. There have just been a few times when I have my class at the college to teach that I've not come to the studio.

Laurie and I have each received separate text messages recently; me from Courtney and her from Maggie. They each asked the same basic, "Are the two of you doing okay?" question. I responded to Courtney with "Sure." I have no idea what Laurie's response to Maggie was... other than Laurie saying that she replied with a "yes." She was, however, typing much longer than just a three-letter answer.

It's been okay. It's been all just work on the songs. Laurie and I seem to be working well enough together to get things done without those people we were in the past getting in our way. It's been... interesting. Any discussion of our past just hasn't happened. Neither of us has said a thing about it being a forbidden topic. Neither of us has brought it up.

This feels different than that night at the alumni gathering. There, we didn't want it brought up since we didn't want to spoil the evening for the others. This is not that. I wonder if she and I are just waiting to see if the other one will mention it. I don't feel as though we are playing a waiting game. At least, I'm not. I'm fine with things as they are; simply working on the songs.

There have been many opportunities for the subject to emerge over the time we've been working here. We are, after all, working with my poems that could provoke a conversation.

Laurie had five songs already for the album. Now, there are the new three. She says there's one... maybe two... of hers that she might put aside for another album. There are a few we are working on now that might fit better with the way the rest of the album is sounding. As a writer, I get that. It's about cohesiveness. The thread of the songs on the album should hold together thematically. If there are songs of a certain style... well, you know.

As I listen to the rhythm of the music for the song we are working on, I look up from my work. As Laurie sits at the table and holds one of the lyric sheets up to read, I can only see her eyes peeking out above the page until she lowers the piece of paper.

Are we being handled?

What?

This whole thing with Derek. For him it's a financial opportunity. I get that. We're paying him a consulting fee. I know what's in it for him. What's in it for us?

I put down the pen and the legal pad that I have in my hands.

Interesting thought. Aside from me getting a percentage for my contribution, his argument about this helping with both of our careers makes sense. That's a compelling reason.

Is that the only reason we're doing this?

That is, indeed, a complicated question. Why are we doing this?

Do you not want to be doing this?

I'm okay with doing this.

So am I. I'm okay with doing this.

Well, then... okay.

We both go back to listening to the instrumental music and looking at our lyric sheets to put together just the right lines in just the right order to complete a song.

There's that pensive look in Laurie's eyes that I see every so often. She brushes her hair back away from her face and tucks it behind her ear. She holds up a poem so I know which one it is, takes a breath, and speaks quietly.

Okay. I told myself that I wasn't going to ask...

Then don't.

Laurie raises an eyebrow at me.

But it's still in here and...

She gestures vaguely in the direction of her head.

Hey, Laurie. I'd like you to look over these...

Devon abruptly enters the workroom. Laurie and I lock eyes. She smiles and shrugs. She places the poem in her hand back in the pile.

Did I interrupt something? I'm ever so sorry.

Laurie, her eyes still locked with mine, responds to Devon without looking over at him.

Yes. I mean, no.

She breaks eye contact with me and looks up at Devon.

I'm sorry. I mean...

Laurie shifts her gaze, for a brief moment, over to me sitting on the floor.

...nothing we can't get back to some other time.

I wonder about that. I wonder about what she was about to ask. I wonder if a truly poignant moment in time has just been lost forever. I wonder if that was our moment, which is now gone.

Are you sure?

Yeah, it's fine. What were you asking about?

Devon looks over at me and then back over at Laurie.

Are the two of you okay?

A look of what I think is exasperation sweeps across Laurie's face.

Yes. We are. And I do wish people would stop asking us that.

Devon starts to back up out the door.

Perhaps I should come back in...

No, Devon, no. No need for that. I apologize. I just got lost in my head for a moment. We can talk about what you need.

Devon steps over to the table with some papers and places them down in front of Laurie. They discuss some music things in the songs. They say things like syncopation... meter... dominant V_7 chord... key of F major. I tune out.

After a few minutes, Devon comes over to me and sits on the floor next to me. He says something about giving Laurie a little bit of time to try something out. We engage in some small talk. I like Devon. He's enjoyable to be around. The kind of guy I would, likely, have become close friends with had we met on our own. We still might become friends. That may depend on how long I will be hanging around the studio. That may also depend on his relationship with Laurie and whatever my relationship with Laurie turns out to be. It's been interesting watching them work together and how Laurie trusts him.

Devon's been very welcoming. I appreciate how he explains music things to me in simple terms without sounding condescending. At least, the things he feels I need to know about. I think he likes the teaching aspect of that. Devon and I have developed some nice camaraderie.

Laurie reaches over to grab her guitar from where it sits leaning against the wall behind her. I watch her face closely as she goes over changes that need to be made to some guitar parts. She tries a few different variations on a particular melody.

My mind drifts back to a memory of watching Laurie's face closely as we sat in our living room while she played her guitar. This is not that woman playing her guitar anymore. And I am not that man watching her anymore. I realize that I have had that thought before. I have verbalized it. But, up until now, it's been an intellectual abstraction. It hits me, for the first time, that we really are just two strangers trying to figure some things out.

Chapter 24
UNTITLED

Given that the lyrics of several more songs have been completed, the others needed a little time to work out some things musically. No need for me to just be hanging around the studio for that. At least until, if and when, Laurie decides if she wants to use any more of my material for any other songs.

Speaking of songs—I settle into my desk chair and click on my rhythm and blues playlist. The opening notes of the first song fill the den. As I shuffle through a stack of my poems, I pull out the pieces I have already dealt with and put those aside.

This is a good day to get wrapped up in stuff for my poetry collection book. I've already put in the poems that are being used for the album. Again, I'm a bit impressed with Derek's ideas. He had the thought that, for the poems that I've altered for use on the album, I include my original versions along with the album versions. I think that is a cool thing to do.

Now I have one stack: the poems that I've already formatted for the book. Mostly, it's the poems that are being used for the album and their new versions. And there are the poems I wrote for Isa that I've already put in. Now I start a second stack: other poems not being used for the album but that I still want included in the book. That was my original deal with Derek—that I would be open to doing this if it wasn't only the poems that were being used as lyrics.

I take a moment to write myself a reminder to text Gen and invite her to the studio. This coming Saturday there will be a little bit of a party there to celebrate the finishing up of a chunk of the album. It seems more like just some reason to have a party. Significant others have been invited as well, so Isa will be there too. Something had been said about Paul and Rowena, Paul and Laurie's daughter, being there.

I thought this would also be a great opportunity to have some outsiders listen to the songs we have so far. Laurie kind of freaked a little at that suggestion. It appears she has this thing about anyone other than the inner circle hearing anything until she feels that they are really ready to be heard.

I'm not sure exactly how it happened, but I was either asked to or I volunteered to bring in some music for our gathering. After all, we have been listening to the same stuff over and over again.

The song on the playlist switches to another. I take that as a cue to scan my music collection to see what I have that would work for a group of music people who have been listening to the same things for a while. Something different. Something out of the ordinary. Something that would be good for a social gathering. Something without lyrics. Something jazzy.

I spot the perfect thing. Keyboard jazz music; good for a

celebration. But in there is also something interesting. Different. Kind of obscure. The music of Jean-Philippe Rameau, an eighteenth-century French composer but played on modern electronic instruments. As music people, I would think they would find it worth listening to. This album was also the one that brings up a memory. A little while after the breakup with Laurie, I discovered this album. For some reason it resonated with me. It made me think of her. But it wasn't a sad feeling. I sent her a copy. It was like, "Hey, I know we aren't together anymore. But I found this piece of music and, well, I just thought you would like it and I wanted to share it with you." I never received a response or even an acknowledgment. I really don't think I expected one. I was hoping for, at least, a "Thank you. I liked it. I hope you are well." Nothing.

Here's one of the poems that would absolutely not work as song lyrics. But I do want it in the book. It's titled *Untitled*. I have no idea at all why I didn't give it a title. I could have at the very least used the first line of the poem as a title. But, no, I didn't do that. I do remember I wrote it when I was very absorbed in the writings of Kahlil Gibran. I took a line from one of his books and it inspired the poem. I might have at the very least used the last line of the poem as a title. It was a line I sort of stole from Shakespeare. But, no, I didn't do that.

Glancing down at the bottom of the page, I see that I had written, "With apologies to those two other guys." I decide that this, sort of, is the new title. But then I think it's just too clunky. Then I see it. There's a better line to use as the title.

Underneath that, I see that I had also scribbled, "one might drown in that ocean."

Chapter 25
ONE MIGHT DROWN IN THAT OCEAN

I am a flute
That the breath of your life
Might pass through

I am a harp
That the touch of your love
Might play on

Sheltered ears that never did hear
Of the symphony of two souls
Awaken to this melody

That would so engage Narcissus
As to have his eyes wander from the pond of his love
To the ocean of ours

As to have him sigh with jealous abandon as he sees
His shallow love cast in shadow
By the light of us
By the tender kiss upon thy tempting lip.

Chapter 26

THIS JUST KEEPS GETTING BETTER AND BETTER

The jazz music plays from the monitors. Intermingled with it are snippets of various conversations. Along with Laurie, Devon, and the three other people who work at the studio, there is a collection of some others. Some of these are significant others. Isa is here. Paul is here. Derek is somewhere in the crowd with Amelia. This collaboration was, after all, his idea.

There is some other family here. Gen is here, as is Rowena, Laurie and Paul's daughter. Although I may be imagining it, there seems to be a moment of Gen and Rowena checking each other out as they meet. A certain flash in their eyes. Awareness and acknowledgment.

These two young ladies have an interesting exchange when they are introduced, and their names are given.

Rowena looks over at her mother and father, across the room, then at me and Isa, then at Gen.

Oh, you have parents like that, too.

Parents like that?

The kind that gives you a name that marks you for life as someone...

Again, Rowena glances over at her parents.

...that is different than anyone else.

Gen looks at us.

Parents that are a few degrees off center? But we love them anyway?

Rowena agrees.

Oh yes.

Gen places her hand on Rowena's arm.

Let's go get some coffee and swap parent stories.

And with that, they both slip off to the break room. I start to give them a word of warning about the coffee but change my mind due to the "few degrees off" comment.

Derek and Amelia appear out of the throng.

Hey, Isaac. Hi, Isabelle. I've had the chance to look at a few of the proofs for your book of poetry.

This comment produces a quizzical look from me.

I'm good friends with a guy from the publishing company. We got together for lunch a few days ago. He brought along the proofs. They look good. Particularly the way your original pieces are presented along with the altered song versions.

Isa and Amelia are having their own conversation, which we can barely hear. I glance over through the open door to the break room. Gen and Rowena are standing by the coffee area involved in their own conversation as well. I notice they both reach for a container of coffee creamer at the same time. Their hands touch, they lean in, and there is a whispered exchange between them. I turn my attention back to Derek.

Thank you. I like this idea a lot.

They are still waiting for a few more of your poems. Ones that aren't being used for songs.

I was about to send them a poem, *Dig*. I wasn't sure

about including it at first. But it's a fun experiment I did with beat poetry. And I have a few others that I'm working on fixing and typing up that I'll send in just a couple of days.

Great.

Our wives are still in the midst of their chat. I notice my Bob James playlist has switched to his Rameau album. There is a change in the atmosphere in the room. This music is quite different than what has been playing. My attention drifts momentarily back to the break room. Gen and Rowena are now giggling about something. They shift and adjust the way they are standing and end up closer to one another.

As Derek and I exchange a few more comments, the chat our wives have been having seems to be coming to its end. Directly over Derek's shoulder, I catch sight of Laurie. She is listening to the Rameau music playing. She looks around at the various people scattered about the room. When she sees me, she has a look on her face that seems to be a look of recognition, like, *I know this. I've heard this before.* I just nod.

Dad?

Gen has come up beside me. Rowena is beside her.

That coffee is not coffee.

Rowena steps closer into us.

I know a place not too far from here. Best coffee. And baklava.

We're going to head out. Enjoy the rest of your celebration gathering. Love you.

Love you.

Gen kisses me and then my wife. Rowena starts to head towards Laurie and Paul.

I'm just going to go say bye to my parents. Be back in a moment.

Rowena moves off. Gen is watching her walk away. She catches me noticing her doing this.

You okay with this?

Is it any of my business?

You know what I mean.

You go and enjoy.

By this time, Rowena has returned.

Okay. I'm all set. Let's go.

With that, Rowena takes Gen's hand. The ladies smile and wave and are off on their journey. I look over at Laurie. She looks over at me. We both shrug at each other.

Derek has a realization of what just happened.

The one with the pink hair is your daughter?

Yes. Genevieve.

I can see that he is working out the details in his head.

And isn't the other one Laurie and Paul's daughter?

Yes. Rowena.

I am thoroughly enjoying the look on Derek's face.

This just keeps getting better and better.

That man just has a damn macabre sense of humor.

Chapter 27
Dig

i dig revelations
the hip kind
the kind that kinda
slap you in the face
with the consciousness
of time and space
and the name
of that red-haired chick
i've been eyeing
i dig a powerful epiphany

Chapter 28
I WILL HOLD YOU TO THAT

ow was your date yesterday?

I click send on my text and put my phone in the phone cradle I have on my desk. Gen rarely responds to texts right away. I fumble with my playlists searching for just the right music for working on some other pieces of poetry for the book.

As I scroll through my albums, I spot the right one and click shuffle. A song begins. I take a moment to enjoy the groove of the rhythm. I ponder the lyrics. My phone dings. Gen's response to my text has come sooner than I thought it would.

It was not a date.

Seriously?

Okay... it did turn into a date. Ro is so interesting.

You're already calling her Ro rather than Rowena? Yeah, that was a date.

Okay, Dad.

What's so interesting about her?

She's just very clear about who she is, and what she wants out of life. That's refreshing after... well, you know.

What do I know?

Dad!

Yes. Okay, I know, I know. Are you seeing her again?

Well, we've already made some plans. So... yes.

Then there is this change in tempo from the previous fairly rapid-fire texts. I can see that Gen is typing something. It goes away. It comes back. She seems to be uncharacteristically hesitant about saying something. Or about how to say it.

At this point, the first song ends and another takes its place. I have a realization about how many songs in my playlists are about broken hearts and relationships gone wrong. It's not a bad thing though. It's a cathartic thing. And they are great songs worth listening to as I write.

I hear a voice in my head. It's not mine. I have a distinct memory of seeing the stage production of *Dreamgirls* on Broadway. I hear Jimmy Early's line, "I can't do it no more. I can't sing no more sad songs."

Finally, my phone dings with Gen's next text.

Are you okay with this?

You asked me that yesterday and I gave you my answer.

But, yesterday, as far as you knew it was only out for coffee. Now it's more... I think... I hope.

Do you get the sense that this is a dangerous person to you, either emotionally or physically?

Hell no. But I'm still not going to be blind to that like I was before, either.

Well, that's good. Then it's still none of my business, is it? Unless you are in danger of being hurt, who you date is none of my business.

But, given whose daughter she is...

I stare at the ellipsis, waiting for Gen to finish her thought with another text. Nothing. I realize she has laid out her thought as much as she is going to. I decide not to keep her in suspense.

You do your thing and I'll do mine.

And what, exactly, is your thing? As far as Ro's mother is concerned?

I'm working with her on a project. That's it.

Have the two of you dealt with your history?

Yes... as much as we need to in order to continue working together efficiently.

A momentary pause in texts. I, again, can see that Gen is typing. I wait.

As much as you really need to or as much as you feel you need to?

Now, that's my girl! Get right to the heart of it. Go for the jugular.

I have trained you well, my young padawan.

You didn't answer the question.

As much as I really need to. I can't speak for Laurie. Are you concerned that my working with Laurie might create problems for you and Rowena?

We like each other. After coffee we...

...and baklava...

...and baklava, we went walking around together for a long time. Just talking. We didn't want the day to end, so then we ended up going out to dinner together. We sat there together. Just talking. And then the restaurant was closing, and we realized that we had been talking for so long that we hadn't even eaten our dinners. We had to have everything wrapped to go.

Yeah. Already calling her Ro? That's a date. Going out to dinner after spending most of the afternoon together? That's a good date. Talking for so long you didn't even eat your dinner? That's a great date.

Don't screw this up for me, Dad, by making things uncomfortable.

When have I ever made things... Never mind. Don't answer that. You have my word.

I will hold you to that. Love you.

Love you. Call my wife.

I will. Bye.

Don't forget about your brother's visit on Wednesday.

I won't. See you all then.

I slip my phone back into its cradle. My playlist changes the song to another "broken hearts and relationships gone wrong" song. I smile and get back to work. I did tell Derek I would send over some of my other poems.

Chapter 29
THE SECRET, THE CANDLE, AND LOVE

The secret,
the silent, searching stares
filled with wonder, longing, and hope.
The candle,
flickering in the moonlight
on the edge of the abyss
at times, almost extinguished, yet
at times burning fierce and steady against the wind,
its light falling across her face in the shadows
gently allowing beauty to illuminate the night.
And love,
always lingering
just beyond grasp,
always drowning
in pale light,
always a fantasy
filled with dreams,
always there,
always love.

Chapter 30
INTERESTING

Our son's presence fills the room. It's not just his physical stature - although his height does tower above me. It's also not that he's very outgoing. He does not seek to be the center of attention. He's an observer. He's a listener. He pays attention. It's not just his piercing green eyes. He's just the kind of man that people are drawn to.

Even though Sam is our youngest, Gen's younger brother, he often gives the impression of being her older brother. She says he's her big brother because he is so much taller than the rest of us. I think she also likes being thought of as the younger sibling.

Of all of my varied accomplishments, I place our having raised two amazing adults as one of our greatest achievements. Their relationship, as sister and brother, is incredibly powerful. They've both, without ever being pressured to follow in either my or Isa's paths, found their own creative force in the world.

We sit together, sprawled out in the living room – he on the couch – me on the floor. The coffee table between us is covered with several piles of papers. Even in this time of electronic files and such, we both still like the feel of the physical paper in our hands.

I look over at our Salvador Dali "dripping clock" wall clock. It never has the correct time. I like that. Very apropos. I do, however, always know exactly by how much it is incorrect.

My wife should be home from work shortly.

Lovely. I think we're done for the evening, anyway.

Let me just check on dinner.

I head into the kitchen and call back to Sam as I do.

I liked many of your suggestions on those poems on top of the other pile we haven't gone over yet. I am going to use most of them. Some of your word choices were better than mine.

Glad I could be helpful. How did you have the time to make notes on my script so quickly? Aren't you working on a multitude of things right now?

I take a moment to think about how many different things I have going on.

Not so much. Yes, there are a few things going on. I'm teaching the class at the college. I'm working on my novel. I'm doing this writing lyrics for an album thing. I'm putting together the book of poetry to go along with the album. I just budget out my time each day to make sure each one of the projects gets my attention. Your script was just as important.

Sam calls back into the kitchen.

Well, papa, I appreciate your comments on the script. That was that scene that I just didn't like the way the dialogue was coming across. Your fixes helped make it sound more natural.

Je vous en prie.

Tish, you spoke French!

Isa had just come through our front door to hear me saying you're welcome to Sam.

That just doesn't have the right feel when you say it, my love.

Je t'en prie, pardonne-moi.

That is better. Tish, you spoke French!

We kiss.

What are you cooking?

That's kakavia. This is stifatho.

Sam's voice comes from the living room.

Papa, you venturing into cooking Mediterranean?

Yes. I'm impressed you know that.

I was dating a woman from Greece.

Of course, you were. You said, "was dating". Things didn't work out?

I want what the two of you have. She wasn't that.

No shame in wanting something better. Just remember to stick with older...

Isa gives me "that look" and raises an eyebrow.

... slightly older...

Try again.

...more mature...

Uh... not quite.

... more seasoned...

What am I? One of your dinners? Nope.

... worldlier...

Worldlier. I like that. Good word choice. Worldlier.

Stick with more worldlier women. Women with experience.

You might have just left it at worldlier.

My wife and I break our embrace and Isa steps into the

living room to greet our son. Mother and son share a warm welcome.

How long are you going to be here for this time?

Just a week. They wanted a few changes in a couple of scenes and a minor character added to one of the scenes. Somebody's girlfriend was promised a role in the movie. I could've just sent them the new pages, but I would rather be on set for a day or two to see how those changes work and combine that with seeing you.

Where's your sister?

She dropped me off earlier this afternoon so dad and I could have some time to work on a few things. Then she went off to spend time with someone. She'll be back here in time for dinner. She should actually be here anytime now.

Splendid. We'll get your room ready after dinner.

You don't have to do that. I'm staying with Gen.

Oh no. You should stay here with us.

My stuff is already there. You're going to be at work during the day. Gen's apartment is closer to the film studio. Papa has his stuff he's working on. Gen and I will come over in the evenings. She's working from home. I want to spend time with her too.

Okay. Fine. As long as you're here by the time I get home.

I will.

I'm going to go change out of my work clothes. How long until dinner, my dear?

Give it maybe another fifteen minutes, if that. Sam, would you set the table please?

You got it.

Isa heads to our bedroom. Sam heads to the kitchen. The doorbell rings.

And also get the door if you would, please. That would be your sister.

Sam greets Gen at the door.

Come on, sis. Help me set the table.

I'm invited to dinner, and you put me to work right away?

Gen places her handbag on the dining room chair and comes into the kitchen to grab some silverware. Sam and Gen chat as they set the table.

That's the way it is. How was your afternoon? Your time with that someone you were going to spend some time with?

Lovely. I was with Ro. I want you to meet her. When it's not going to be an awkward "meeting the family" thing.

Too soon for that?

Maybe. No. I don't know. Just being cautious.

I enter the conversation.

I have been warned to not screw this up for her.

Sam pauses setting the plates down and looks over at Gen.

Oh really? That serious?

It could be. I don't yet, exactly. It feels right.

Are you dating each other just to freak out both sets of parents?

That thought did cross our minds.

At this, I stop fussing with dinner and look out through the opening between the kitchen and dining room.

Seriously?

No. Not at all, dad. Absolutely not. That's not what this is.

Gen turns toward her Sam and speaks in mock sotto voce.

Although we did joke about that when we were having dinner together.

I interject.

Joking implies something is funny.

Dad, you do like saying that don't you?

Only when something is decidedly not funny.

Sam finishes this conversation.

The dinner together where you didn't have dinner?

That did, indeed, finish that conversation.

Brother and sister finish with their task and sit in the living room chatting. A few moments later Isa emerges from our bedroom, gives our daughter a kiss, and joins them in their chat. My phone dings. I see it's a text from Laurie.

Now this is interesting.

Isa poses a question.

How interesting?

Laurie wants me to send her "Return of the Night Visitor". It's not one that I gave to her but it's one of the pieces that I want in the book. She's heard about it from Derek, and she has a thought about using it. Okay, if that's what they want. I'll send it to her tomorrow.

Now Sam poses a question.

Why is that so interesting?

It's not a poem. It's sort of a very brief short story. It's not a song lyric kind of thing. They have an idea about using it for a spoken word thing with music underneath it.

Gen shares her opinion.

That could be interesting.

Yes... interesting. Oh, and dinner's ready.

Chapter 31
THE RETURN OF THE NIGHT VISITOR

trange... how strange to feel the night breathe. Moonlight, abandoned by the moon, finds its way to and presses against my window. The moonlight leaks through the window and drips down on my forehead. Startled, I jump... awake... alone. Strange. I could have sworn that I was sharing my bed with someone. Not just someone. Her. Always her. But, as usual, no one's head peeks out from beneath the too-big-for-one-person covers. No one has been stealing my pillow.

Trying to reorient myself, I run my fingers through my now soaking wet hair. The sweat comes off in my hand, iridescent in the light of... four A.M.? Is that what the clock says? Yes, that is what the clock says. Its numbers blazing in the dark corner of my room.

In the corner... moonlight playing tricks on me. It can't be her, but... it looks like her. No. Just my eyes playing tricks on me. And my nose. I could swear that scent is one I have inhaled often. Not a perfume. No. The scent of her... her skin.

I have to turn away... close my eyes... throw my head

into the pillow. I don't use my pillow to sleep on. I use it for moments like this. I use it to try to shut out all these thoughts... try to shut out her. The room is suddenly cold but there's this warmth that I can sense. It's a familiar warmth. I feel it move around the bed, closer to me, closer to what was once her side of the bed.

Leaping up, I hear my voice scream, "Why can't you leave me the hell alone? Let me sleep! Let me be! I love you! Leave me alone!"

The apparition moves away from this outburst. My desk gets in the way of her retreat. A single piece of paper is separated from the others and floats noiselessly to the floor, passing through a streak of moonlight, the writing on it high-lighted for that brief moment in eternity. My night visitor moves to retrieve what was lost. Her eyes scan the lines of the poem that was meant for the memory of her. She places it, ever so delicately, back in the spot from whence it came and turns toward me.

Her eyes gaze into mine and I weaken. She moves to the bed, lies next to me, and pulls the covers around her... a familiar move. The warmth feels so wonderful I find myself putting my arms around the apparition and pulling it closer. My skin melts together with hers as the warmth lulls me to a long-awaited deep sleep.

Strange... how strange to feel the night breathe.

Chapter 32
SEPARATE TABLES, PLEASE

The following Saturday morning has been spent at the studio working out some details about using "The Return of the Night Visitor" for the album. It does have an interesting feel to it. We've changed the gender pronouns. Since Laurie is the one performing it, the night visitor is now a male figure. The music that Laurie has written for it most definitely adds to its mood nicely.

I have never really been a fan of the spoken word thing on a music album. This, however, seems to work. Perhaps it's because it's the entire piece being done that way and not simply a bit of dialogue just stuck in an otherwise lyrical piece. And it's not really being spoken – but not quite sung. Laurie's done a fascinating job with it.

I look over at the clock on the workroom wall.

It would be good to take a break from this shortly. Isa is meeting me here very soon so we can go to lunch together.

Devon also looks up at the clock.

A break soon would be good.

Laurie checks her phone for a text message.

And Paul is also stopping by for lunch.

I gather up the notes I've been working on.

I just want to write a few more things down while they're still in my head.

My phone and Laurie's phone ding almost at the same time. We both check our messages.

Oh. Paul just letting me know that Ro is with him.

Both our children are also with Isa. They'll be here in a few minutes. You haven't met our son, Sam, yet.

I'm looking forward to that.

Laurie and I exchange looks. I think we both realize that was probably the first pleasant, personal, simply conversational, non-work-related thing that has been said between us.

We are just about done clearing everything up and turning off whatever needs to be turned off. Two of the other studio people have already left to go get their lunch. A few of the others are getting something to eat from the breakroom fridge. Paul and Rowena come into the studio. Greetings are exchanged. Then Isa, Gen, and Sam enter the studio. Some more greetings are tossed around. Gen and Ro greet each other very warmly. There are glances between me, Isa, Laurie, and Paul. Laurie is the one to speak up first.

Well, should we all go out for lunch now?

I nod in agreement.

Sure. I'll meet you back here in about an hour and a half?

There are some more pensive glances around the quartet. I have to ask the question.

Oh. When you said all, did you mean all of us?

I might have.

As in all of us together?

I think I did. Maybe.

The younger trio is watching this, thoroughly enjoying this moment of awkwardness. Devon, who has been standing in the doorway of the breakroom, has also been watching this whole thing.

Paul takes control of the situation.

Yes. Let's all go out to lunch... together.

There is a moment of hesitation.

Paul offers another thought.

I insist. We should spend, at least, a little time together. Our daughters are, after all... you know.

The trio looks at each other. Gen offers a suggestion.

Separate tables for the generations, okay?

Chapter 33
SEPARATE CHECKS, PLEASE

The restaurant that Laurie has suggested is not too far from the studio. It's one of those quaint little places tucked into a spot off the street in a courtyard where you wouldn't expect there to be a restaurant. There's a pleasant mix of different cuisines on the menu. Quite a few patrons scattered about, but not too many people. A typical lunchtime crowd. There's some fun, eighties music playing.

The younger trio has gotten their request for a separate table. After pulling out a chair for Isa, I sit across from her and can see the kids over her left shoulder. The body language between Gen and Rowena is intense. At the moment, the ladies have their hands on each other's thighs, but Rowena is leaning in towards Sam. She and Sam seem to be enjoying getting acquainted. Gen is just watching their connection happen. Lots of smiling. Some giggling.

The elder quartet has been sitting fairly quietly. We seem to be more absorbed in the menu choices rather than any conversation between us. Our waitress, Tonya, has already placed four glasses of water on the table and has gone off with our other drink orders.

The ambient sound of various conversations joins with the clattering of utensils, plates, and glasses. Floating just underneath that is the background music. Our table is, however, fairly quiet. A few questions have been tossed across the square table. Isa has asked if I am going to have the salmon. Paul has said the menu has a beef burgundy dish and asked Laurie if she would like to try it. Stuff like that. The sound of laughing coming from the trio's table catches my attention. They may be having a better time than we are. Tonya arrives with our drinks. I've opted for a Grey Goose dirty martini with two olives. Isa has a whiskey sour. Paul has ordered whiskey on the rocks. Laurie has a Wild Huckleberry Mint Mojito. Tonya takes our food orders.

Paul offers a toast.

Here's to... hell, I don't know. Here's to whatever this all turns out to be.

Again, there's an outburst of laughter from the trio's table. I can still see them over Isa's shoulder. The other three turn to look over at them. We turn our attention back to ourselves, clink our glasses, and drink. Silence ensues.

Laurie breaks this silence.

Isabelle, how long have you and Isaac been together?

This leads into some basic exchange of information. Such as how long each couple has been together and where each couple met. Most of this is the domain of the women. Until...

Paul interjects with a question. He looks at me and then at Laurie.

And how did the two of you meet?

Oh. I guess we're going to go there.

I know some things. You were together in college. And I know how long you were together and about the breakup. But I'm interested in knowing some more details.

Why?

Good question, Laurie.

Whatever happened between you and this guy here...

Paul points across the table at me.

Isaac.

I apologize. This guy, Isaac, was involved in your life before I was. I don't really know too much about that time of your life. So, I'm intrigued. What about you, Isa? Do you know everything you want to?

Oh, I'm sorry—Isaac is the only one who calls me Isa. And, yes, I do.

Fair enough... Isabelle.

Bits and pieces of our past are offered up. Laurie and I met at a theatre party. We choreographed some pieces together for the dance company. We worked on a production together. We took a Shakespeare class together and performed a duet scene. We parented a cat together. Nothing too in-depth or vastly personal. Just filling in some of the blanks for Paul until his curiosity seems satisfied. It's really mostly the same things that were brought up during the alumni reunion gathering.

Tonya arrives with our lunches. Dishes are placed around the table. Tonya sets a plate of Tuscan ravioli in front of Isa and begins to move away. She stops and turns back to the table.

Would you like some sprinkle cheese with that?

Excuse me? Some what?

Tonya holds out a serving container of grated parmesan cheese... also known as, by Tonya, as sprinkle cheese.

Oh, yes please.

Tonya places the sprinkle cheese on the table.

Would the table like another round of drinks?

Oh, yes please.

Isa and Paul wait until Tonya is no longer within hearing distance and burst into laughter. Laurie and I do find the moment funny. But Isa and Paul find this quite hilarious.

Oh, the poor girl. Does she just not know the word parmesan?

Isa and Paul share another few moments of giggling about the sprinkle cheese comment. They share comments like, "Maybe that's just what she calls parmesan," and "Perhaps she thinks she's being funny," and "Well, damn, she was funny." Laurie and I just begin eating our lunches and watch this strange bonding between the two of our spouses transpire.

Isabelle, what's your thing?

My thing?

Your thing. What you do.

Oh. I'm an interior designer.

That is wonderful. I have some questions for you. I'm an art director for a magazine. I have some thoughts about a project that I'm planning that I've always wanted to have an interior designer's ideas about.

This launches Isa and Paul into quite an intense, lively conversation. Some time goes by. There is another outburst of laughter from the trio's table. Laurie and I look at each other. There is the acknowledgment that we are both just sitting there and definitely not part of our spouses' conversation. We sit quietly enjoying our lunches. Eventually, Tonya comes over with our second round of drinks.

Isa looks up at Tonya and hands her the container of parmesan.

I'm done with the sprinkle cheese. Thank you.

As soon as Tonya is far enough away from our table, Isa and Paul again erupt into laughter about this. And then back they go into their discussion of interior design.

I must have had a strange look on my face, which causes Isa to interrupt her conversation with Paul.

What is it? You have that look in your eyes.

What look?

That look you get when you're chasing some idea in your head.

It's the music. A piece of an old memory. There was a dance club in our college town. It was called The Fleetwood. This was a song they played often. We went there quite a bit my freshman year.

And just who did you go dancing with? Who is this we?

There was this woman from my fencing class.

Isa turns to Paul.

Well, Paul, I guess I didn't know everything I wanted to.

After having sat in silence for quite a while, Laurie seizes the opportunity to join the conversation.

I don't remember The Fleetwood.

It had changed owners and names several times.

Another memory emerges. Isa turns to Paul.

There is that look again. He's very cute when he's chasing an idea in his head. Especially when he's writing. He gets this distant, far-off look in his eyes.

Cute? I would have thought I stopped being cute thirty years ago. Cute?

Sexy. I meant to say sexy. But you'll always be cute, as well as sexy.

Isa turns to Laurie.

This is as good a time as any to say this. This may not

come out right... but what the hell. Thank you for breaking up with Isaac. If you know what I mean.

I do know what you mean. I think.

There's a little bit more conversation about the college town between Laurie and me. There's a little bit more conversation about interior design between Isa and Paul. Tonya has been by to collect our empty plates and glasses. We ask for our checks. I look over at the trio's table. They seem to be finishing up as well. Tonya appears at our table again.

I'm kinda embarrassed about this and I hope I don't offend anyone.

Tonya sighs.

You asked for separate checks. But—and I'm really sorry about this—I'm not sure who is with who here. I've been watching the table to see if I could figure out who the couples are. But I can't.

We completely understand Tonya's predicament. We do our best to make sure that she does not feel bad about this. Although, I am curious.

Tonya, just out of curiosity... what were your thoughts about who is with who here?

Tonya immediately turns an interesting shade of red.

Oh, I wouldn't want to presume.

It's okay. Go ahead and presume. I'm a writer and I think this would make an interesting part of a story.

Well... if you don't mind...

Laurie, it seems, is also curious.

We don't mind. Go ahead.

Tonya looks first at Isa then at Paul.

Well, the two of you looked like you were having a great time and enjoying your conversation with each other. So, I thought you might be a couple.

She looks at Laurie and then me.

But the two of you didn't seem like you were a couple at all. That's what got me a little confused. The two of you weren't interacting much at all. And then I thought maybe the women were together and the guys were together. But then, after a while, I saw that that didn't make much sense either. And then I couldn't tell...

I gently interrupt and thank Tonya for her candor. We explain what should be on each check and hand over our credit cards. Tonya goes off to do her thing. Paul clears his throat.

So, here's a question I have. Given what our lovely server just said... that the two of you didn't seem like you were a couple at all. I get that you're working together on Laurie's album. And she has said that things in the studio are going well. Given all that—and this is not a jealousy thing—at least I don't think it is—how do the two of you feel about each other now? I don't mean about working together. I get that the two of you have found a way to deal with a working relationship that apparently is working for you both. I mean, given your past, and then your paths crossing again, how do you feel about each other now?

I look over at Laurie. I study her face to figure out what she might be thinking about this query. I wonder which one of us is going to offer a response first. She nods to defer to me.

I would say... and I don't mean to speak for you, Laurie, but I believe you would agree with me on this... when you are younger and in a relationship, you may have the impression that what you're feeling—about the depth of your feeling—that this is all there is, that this is the total depth of love that you are capable of. As we experience other relationships, and we have deeper connections...

I look over at Isa.

...we come to the realization that what we were feeling when we were younger is nowhere near the depth of feeling about another person, the depth to which you may truly bond with another, that we are capable of. We don't know the intensity of a true connection because we haven't experienced it yet.

I then look over at Laurie.

And I don't, in any way, mean to belittle or demean our relationship, but you and I—we just skimmed the surface... and those ripples have since faded away.

I now look over at Paul.

So, Paul, to answer your question, and I understand you didn't want a response about our working relationship, but that is basically all it is. I can't say that I feel anything about Laurie other than I am enjoying working on this creative project. I might feel the same if it was almost anyone else that I was working with. This is actually the very first time, since the alumni reunion, that we've even spent any time together outside the studio.

I pause to let the others process this.

And now, let us ask Laurie if she would agree.

I would say I would agree with that.

Here's the more interesting question. If Laurie and I had never met in college and never had a relationship—if our paths crossed now, for the first time—would we have any kind of connection? Now, that is a profound question.

And what is the answer to that profound question?

There is no possible way to know that. Laurie and I did have a relationship. We can't deny that. It's part of us. It's ingrained in us. It altered the course of our life paths. And if we had never met before, we'd be different people. Even though our past relationship doesn't affect us anymore, it did have an indelible effect on the relationships we now have. And that's a nice thing.

We all agree that that is, indeed, a good thing.

Yes. It is.

Tonya arrives back at our table with our credit cards and bill to finish up. She, again, apologizes for the confusion. We, again, reassure her it was fine, and tell her she helped us figure something out a little. This leaves her with a confused look on her face. We leave her a very nice tip. I look past Isa's shoulder to see that the younger trio is also finishing taking care of their bill with their server.

And here's the next important phase of our new relationship... relationships. Our daughters are in a relationship of their own. Our lives are likely going to be intertwined whether we like it or not.

I look up and watch as the younger trio steps over to our table.

You kids have a good time?

Lovely. We're going to start walking back. We'll meet you at the cars.

We watch as Gen takes Rowena by one hand and Sam by the other. They create a little bit of a scene as they attempt to get through the restaurant door still all hand in hand, giggling as they exit.

We start to gather our things to make our own exit as well. Paul reaches out to shake my hand. I respond in kind. Not satisfied with a simple handshake, he then moves in for a hug. Apparently, he's a hugger. He then moves toward Isa with his arms out. He pauses and looks at me.

May I?

Thank you for asking. But you need to ask Isa that question.

Isa and Paul share a brief but meaningful hug. Upon

the release of said hug, Isa and Laurie move in for an ever-so-slightly hesitant hug as well. Isa and Paul stare at Laurie and me expectantly.

Well?

May I?

I insist.

Laurie and I acquiesce, and we both move in to exchange a hug. It all becomes a complete mess. Our arms end up in all the wrong places—we both go low. We both tilt our heads to the same side and collide a bit.

After our giggling has subsided a little, Laurie offers a suggestion.

Dinner and drinks next Saturday night? Your place? I'd love to see your home... good way to get to know you a little more.

Chapter 34
BACK TO WORK

The walk back to the studio was quite interesting. Still some remnants of the conversation between Isa and Paul going on. We start out walking alongside our spouses. Laurie and Paul, having exited the restaurant first, are slightly ahead of us. The kids are already far out of sight. As we walk and Paul continues to question Isa about various ideas, Paul slows down. Isa speeds up. They end up walking with each other as their discussion goes on. Laurie has shifted her position and is now walking just behind them. I am walking just behind Laurie.

There is this unspoken thing going on between me and Laurie about whether or not we are going to walk next to each other. Does she slow down? Do I speed up? She's partially listening to the exchange between Isa and Paul. She's partially paying attention to our relative positions. Every so often she glances back at me. Perhaps the attempted hug in the restaurant was a little too much for us.

Eventually we come around the corner to find the kids in front of the studio. They have been giggling, yet again, about something. When they see us, they all give us huge waves.

The spouses exchange "see you later" comments. Plans for getting together at our place the following Saturday are confirmed. Laurie and I bid farewell to the kids. Gen and Rowena share a kiss. Rowena asks Gen to call her later. Rowena then gets in the car with her dad. Gen, Sam, and Isa head down the street, get in the car, and both cars move off.

After all the excitement of lunch, conversation, our encounter with Tonya—Laurie and I now find ourselves alone with each other again. There's a moment—not really awkward—the awkwardness of this whole thing has passed. It's more of a what our next step is going to be moment.

I figure the next step should be me holding the door of the studio open for Laurie to go in. I follow.

Devon and the others have already returned to the studio from lunch and appear to be quite busy setting knobs and dials, plugging this thing into that thing, and so on. When he sees us, Devon stops his fiddling around on the control board.

How was your lunch with the whole crew? First time with the four of you?

It was fine. I think we all got along just fine. Especially Paul and Isaac's wife. They had quite a good time together.

Devon smiles, nods, reaches into his pocket, pulls out two five-dollar bills, and extends the money toward Laurie. I glance questioningly at the money in Devon's hand.

Here. Then I guess I owe you this.

Laurie takes the money and pockets it. Devon moves off to another part of the studio.

What was that all about?

Devon bet me ten dollars that this whole thing would

eventually crash and burn, and you and I would be having issues with each other all the time.

Seriously?

I call down to the other end of the studio where Devon is now sitting.

Oh, Devon. I am so disappointed in you. Never bet against me, Devon!

I got it wrong. Not ashamed to admit that. Ever so pleased about that though. However, it was not you I was actually concerned about.

Laurie grabs an empty package of some sort of tech thing that is sitting on the console and flicks it toward Devon. It hits him on the shoulder and then it clatters to the floor.

You deserved that.

I suppose I did.

Laurie leans against the door to the workroom. Her hair falls over her eyes. She brushes it away from her face and tucks it back behind her ears.

Devon had a point though. A bunch of people—my husband, your wife, our kids, our friends—have probably all been wondering what has been going on in here.

Let's go sit down.

I gesture inside the workroom. Laurie and I enter, and I close the door behind us. We circle around the table. I pull out a chair for her and then sit across from her.

Ooh—not sitting on the floor? This must be serious.

No. Not serious. We're just going to have a conversation and me sitting up here, rather than the floor, is better for eye contact.

A conversation about what?

Pick a topic.

What?

Just pick a topic. We're back in each other's lives again. Let's just get to know each other.

Okay. I'm pleased about the way the album is coming...

No. Not about the album. Not about our past either. Let's just talk.

I'm not sure where to...

I have no idea what happened to you after college. What did you do?

Traveled around a bit. Singing in all kinds of little clubs. Any bar with a performance space. Places like that.

Alone or with a band?

Well, there wasn't any band. After a while.

What happened?

Things just never came together. Or, more precisely, they did come together. Just not in a good way.

I assume that there's more to this story.

Laurie leans forward with her chin resting on her hands. She looks directly at me and cocks her head to one side.

Well, if you really want to know...

We're having a discussion. We're just getting to know each other again.

Well, okay. We didn't have a manager. I mean, we couldn't get a manager. So, we decided to manage ourselves. That's when all the real fighting started.

She rises from her chair and heads over to a small cabinet sitting in the corner. I noticed it there the first time I was in the room but never thought much about what was in it.

We each now seemed to want to play different types of music. We each thought we knew best how to make the group more successful.

She opens the cabinet, takes out two glasses and a bottle of Glenlivet.

And we all cared far too much about our own original songs and far too little about each other's. That's when we realized we needed one of us to be in charge of making all the decisions.

After pouring the scotch into the glasses, she strides over into the break room and opens the freezer.

And who got the job?

We couldn't decide. I mean, we could decide. Five band members. Five different decisions of who should be in charge. We each wanted to be in control. To make everything more difficult there were these factions in the group. I was good friends with the keyboard player, but the bassist was good friends with the drummer. The other guitarist just wanted to stay out of the whole thing but also didn't want any of us others making the decisions. Stalemate.

She tosses some ice into the glasses, steps back into the workroom. She comes up behind me and leans over my chair to place a glass in front of me. She then swings around the table and sits back down in her chair.

I guess a democracy was out of the question.

Oh, yes. Definitely out of the question. Our egos wouldn't allow that.

So, what did you do?

The conversation pauses for a moment as Laurie gestures for us to clink our glasses. We do. As we sip from our glasses, I look at Laurie over the top of my glass, waiting for a response to my question.

None of us knew what to do. While all this fighting was going on, I was performing solo wherever I could. Our drummer ended up getting a gig as a session drummer in a recording studio. The keyboard player decided that they were going to collaborate with someone else to write, in his words, the next great rock musical. The bassist got a tour with another band, so she quit. And the other guitarist started sitting in for the guitarist of another band who was in rehab. We kept rehearsing together until our other schedules and commitments took over and then we just stopped working together.

That's too bad. It would have been nice to have something like that work out better for you. How splendid that things did eventually work out and you were able to have your first album and now a second one.

I really believe you mean that.

Of course, I do. I know how much your music means to you... how fulfilled it makes you.

There. You did it again!

Did what?

You said something nice to me. I mean, something just really thoughtful and nice. Just simply spoke to me.

I did. Didn't I?

Yes. You did.

Should I do it again?

If you think you can handle it.

I don't know... I think I can.

Great. You ready?

Yes. Here we go...

Silence.

It doesn't work if you force it, huh?

I guess not. But it was worth a try.

That was nice though, wasn't it?

What was nice? You mean what I said?

Yes. We had a nice moment there.

Is that what they call a moment?

I suppose.

I had a moment? I mean, we had a moment?

Yes.

Wow. I've always wanted to have a moment.

And now you've had one.

I'm glad you were with me when I had my moment. I mean, I'm glad I had my moment with you.

Just stop saying moment.

Got it.

I take a sip from my glass.

But that wasn't thirty years of your life.

No. After the band imploded, I did the solo singer/songwriter thing for a little while. Wasn't able to make a living at it. I tried to figure out what I really wanted to do with my life. A friend got me a job at an international trade company. It was okay. Dealing with purchase documents, transportation documents, bills of lading. Pretty boring stuff. I wasn't really meant for the business office lifestyle. But I liked connecting with people in all these foreign countries. Did that for a long time. Still played the occasional set in a bar when I could. Open mic nights. I met and fell in love with Paul. Paul inspired me to really dedicate myself back into writing and playing music. Had three lovely children along the way.

Why have I not heard anything about other kids? Oh, wait... one just graduated from college?

Recently. Yes. How did you know that? Oh, that Facebook post a while ago. That's right. Natalia is in Europe. Post-graduation backpacking travel trip thing. She'll be back soon. And we have a son, Raphael, our oldest.

I must have had a far-off look in my eyes. A look which prompted a question from Laurie.

What are you thinking?

I was just... I find it very interesting and kind of

groovy that we... you and I... after years... many years... at this later phase of our lives... ended up where we are. I wrote poetry and plays. Never thought of myself as a novelist...

...or a lyricist.

...or a lyricist. I was just thinking that it's rather cool that —not that we're old—but at this older part of our lives we're still...

...exploring new opportunities.

Well put.

Laurie leans forward, puts her arm on the table and rests her cheek in her palm.

What about you? What happened to you?

You mean, after college?

I know about grad school. I was with you when you got your acceptance letter.

Yes, you were. Let's see. After grad school I was offered a job in a puppet touring company. One of a group manipulating the marionettes and doing the voices.

That's something you would be good at.

But I turned it down to take a teaching position. Seemed like the right thing to do at the time. I taught for quite a while. Balanced teaching and doing theatre. Directed theatre productions. Acted every once in a while, when the right role came up. Met Isa doing a theatre production. Married. Had two wonderful kids. Then I got an idea for a novel and delved into that. And then kept writing more.

Laurie takes a sip from her glass.

Well, that's all very nice. For a man who usually packs a whole lot of stuff into just a few words, you've managed to tell me very little. You haven't told me anything about you.

If you really want to know...

We're having a discussion. We're just getting to know each other again.

We both smile at her using my own words against me.

Fair enough.

I sip again from my glass.

I wandered through life aimlessly for a little while. Oh, I was busy enough. I finished grad school. I was teaching. I was performing and directing in regional theatres. But I felt like I was only just doing stuff. I was doing... not being. I had stopped writing. Didn't feel as though I had anything left to write about.

Because of me?

Well... yes. But what happened between us was just the initiating incident. I was... evolving. The romantic in me would, of course, love to give Isa all of the credit... to say that my meeting Isa changed my life... which it did. She's, most definitely, a vital part of my transformation. But there was a step before that. That step made me into the man that Isa would fall in love with.

And what was that step?

I'm going to try to not get all spiritual and mystical here. And I don't think I can really put it into words that would make any sense to anyone other than me. The closest I can get is... I was broken. I was shattered. I looked at the scattered shards of who I was. I took all the pieces that I truly needed to rid myself of. I crushed them into dust and let them go. I took all the pieces that I truly needed to hold on to. I nurtured them.

I pause momentarily to let Laurie process what I just said.

Those were good words, Isaac. I do understand. And I appreciate you opening up to me like that.

And then I found my path. In the most unlikely of places.

And where was that?

Sorry. That's my own to hold sacred.

I get that. I respect that. Okay.

I am often very open about just about everything in my life... but not that. I'm not trying to be cagey here, but you must allow me my little touch of mysteriousness.

We both take another sip of our drinks. I then finish my thought.

But my path was revealed. My path became illuminated. Along that path there was Isa. I met this gentle soul with the universe in these fathomless eyes. I was healed. And now, here we are.

Laurie raises her glass.

Yes. Here we are.

Glasses clink. We drink.

And now our daughters have found each other. Their paths have crossed.

Yes, they have. That's an interesting situation.

Yes, Laurie, it is.

Perhaps that is what all of this is about.

We finish the contents of our glasses.

Well, Isaac, back to work?

No more chatting?

Let's not overdo it. Back to work.

Chapter 35
JUST SO COOL

We rescheduled our dinner together, at our place, for the following Tuesday. Sam is flying back to L.A. tomorrow and the kids wanted to be all together again before he had to leave.

Conversation around the dinner table has involved Gen and Rowena sharing their plans for a weekend trip away together to visit Sam in three weeks. The idea that their relationship is something more than just dating sinks in a bit more.

Dinner time has also been spent involved in some great conversation about the Beatles. We did have some Beatles music playing earlier in the evening. The playlist is now some sixties and seventies soul.

Our living room contains quite a bit of Beatles paraphernalia. Posters, figurines, mugs, commemorative plate, all of the music albums—group and solo stuff—and all of the movies—group and solo stuff—are part of the décor. Paul, also a Beatles fan, enjoyed checking out our bookcase, over in the den, filled with a plethora of Beatles-related books. Paul is also intrigued by the display of all my swords that are on the den walls. Some of these are remnants of my directing productions of *Romeo and Juliet* and *Hamlet*. Others are thoughtful gifts.

I've been bonding a bit with an ex-girlfriend's husband.

We've finished dinner and I start to clear the table.

I have some exciting news to share.

Sam waits until he has everyone's attention.

I didn't want to say anything until all the arrangements were taken care of. My lease is up at the end of the month. Since I can do my screenwriting from anywhere... I've decided to move back here.

Isa leaps up to hug our son.

That is exciting! It will be wonderful to have you back here and to spend more time with you. We'll prepare your room.

Sam breaks his embrace with his mother.

When I said back here... I didn't mean back here in this house. I'm going to get my own place. I've found an apartment. Not too far from the house. But not too close. I promise we'll get together for dinners here every weekend. I'll fill you in on all the details a little later.

Isa is a little disappointed but still pleased.

And since Gen and Ro are visiting...

Sam looks over at the ladies.

...I'll have plenty of help packing up. Won't I?

The ladies agree.

Gen and Ro giggle a bit.

We'll have a great time.

I raise my glass and propose a toast.

To wonderful family times ahead. It will be lovely to have all of us together again. And, I believe, Laurie and Paul's daughter, Natalia, will also be back home from Europe shortly.

Laurie puts on a look of mock panic.

Oh no. Let's not introduce Natalia to Sam. That would just be too weird.

Awkward silence. Exchanged glances.

I was joking.

A few more moments of silence. Rowena breaks it.

Joking implies something was funny.

I start laughing.

Oh, I like this woman.

I turn my attention to Gen.

Did you tell Rowena to say that?

I did not tell her to say that. Only that you say it.

Oh, I like this woman even more.

Sam takes this as his cue.

Tell me more about Natalia. Anyone have a picture?

Dinner, a Beef Daube Provençale with Bandol Red Wine, is in the process of being cleared away. The elder quartet has been busy cleaning up and moving things from the dining room table to the kitchen to be dealt with. We've told our children to get out of our way and spend some time together.

The younger trio sits on one of the couches in the living room. They have pulled out some of our scrapbooks and have been sharing some childhood photos and stories with one another. Gen is telling a story about my reading *Charlotte's Web* to her when she was a little girl, perhaps four years old. The rest of us have been listening to this.

...and then Dad gets to the part where Fern is in school, but she's thinking about Wilbur and not paying any attention to the teacher. Until the teacher asks Fern what the capital of Pennsylvania is... and she says, "Wilbur." And I say to Dad that I know what the capital of Pennsylvania is.

Gen stops her story and calls to me through the opening between the dining room and the kitchen.

And what did you say then, Dad?

I didn't realize that this was an audience participation thing.

Well, it has to be told right.

I said, "Really, Gen? You know what the capital of Pennsylvania is? That is wonderful. And what is the capital of Pennsylvania? And you said... go ahead... finish it."

I said the capital of Pennsylvania is P. And then my dad says...

"Gen, you have a very interesting way of looking at the world."

To which I reply...

Without missing a beat.

...without missing a beat, I reply, "How can I look at the world if I'm in the world?"

Laurie pauses as she is helping put some of the remains of dinner in the refrigerator and looks over at me.

So very precocious. That is so your child.

My playlist switches songs. As if on cue, everything suddenly turns into the cleaning-up-dinner scene from *The Big Chill*. I grab a platter—and Isa—and, balancing the platter on one hand like a server, we tango over to the kitchen counter... and dip. Paul has grabbed a bowl—and Laurie—and waltzed over to the sink. The four of us dance out to the dining room, pick up some glassware, and dance back toward the kitchen.

We all get a bit clumped at the entrance to the kitchen. After we all separate to get through the opening, I find myself now dancing with Laurie. I glance over to see Isa dancing with Paul.

The glassware gets placed in the dishwasher and we

regroup to our original partners. The music carries us back out to the dining room for the last bits of silverware and such.

The younger trio has been watching this in stunned silence. The song comes to an end and each of them have their own reaction.

Gen: Well... that was interesting.

Rowena: They are so odd. Who started that? Did my parents infect your parents... or the other way around?

Sam: Who cares? That was... just so cool.

Chapter 36
WE'RE ON IT

...**A**nd Sam and Rowena just bonded immediately. It was like they were old friends right away. It was nice to see them get along so well.

Isa is finishing sharing the events of the last few days with the group. This time it's Ric and Gabriel's turn to host. Although Ric is the one who runs a restaurant, Gabriel is trying a steak with elderberry mustard recipe. Ric, however, has made a point to set out a few bottles of the cabernet that we liked because he says it pairs nicely with the dinner.

Olivia, as usual, is flitting around refilling wine glasses and passing around hors d'oeuvre platters. As she comes back over to the group, she takes a moment to place a hand on Isa's shoulder.

And when did he go back?

Sam flew back to L.A. on Wednesday. I am missing him already. But he'll be back soon.

Ric leans forward to place his wine glass on the coaster on the coffee table.

It's true. Our children are not ours for very long.

He gestures over to the framed photographs of his and Gabriel's two adopted children set on top of the piano. Gabriel calls out from the kitchen.

And they never call us as much as we would like them to.

And then he adds—with just a little touch of mock sorrow—

Break my heart.

Matt joins in the conversation.

Our kids haven't visited since last holiday time. And that was far too brief a visit. Em and I have tried to arrange more time with everyone. They're just so busy with their own kids. It's difficult with everyone's schedules.

Keli responds to this.

Everyone's schedules are crazy. Gene and I try to do, at least, birthdays with ours. It just keeps getting harder and harder. Then you miss one birthday, and it doesn't seem like a big deal. You say we'll do it some other time. But then you miss another one.

Olivia and Akiva have chosen to remain childless but add to the group's thoughts.

Can't say that we know how you feel. But I do remember being the ones who were young and not calling or seeing our parents as much as they wanted us to.

Isn't that the tragic part of it? As much as they wanted us to? We should have wanted to... too.

I decide that we have had enough of this cloud of parental despondency.

Alright. I miss spending time with Sam as well. That just makes me appreciate the time we do have together even more. I'll be the one to say it. Even though I do miss having the kids around as much as we once did, I love that it's just Isa and me again after all these years.

Isa smiles at me.

That is nice. And we can walk around naked all the time.

Akiva raises a question.

All the time?

Well, not when I'm cooking. I do wear an apron for that.

Isa interjects.

But only an apron. Otherwise... naked.

I get back to our topic of discussion.

For a long time, our relationship was only about being Dad and Mom and raising the kids. Now we're back to being husband and wife and the relationship we had before kids. We...

Isa interrupts my thought.

Ah... not quite the same relationship that we had before the kids.

Why not the same?

Because it's better. We're closer now because of what we went through raising children. And we appreciate each other more.

I turn back to the group.

So, there you have it. Better.

Being the gracious host that he is, Ric takes control.

Okay. Change of topic. Akiva. Your serve.

Akiva momentarily looks a little surprised. He quickly composes himself.

Fine. Isaac. How's your book of poems coming along?

Now it's my turn to look a little surprised.

I haven't really thought about it much while we've been working in the studio. I do need to get some more of the poems to the publisher soon. They're doing this cool thing where they have my original poem set next to the song version. I like that. But I do need to get back to that project.

Is the album done?

I don't know. It's not for me to say. It's not my gig. There are times that it seems done and the others are dealing with bass parts, background vocals, and recording things.

And other times?

And other times, someone comes up with an idea to fix something or add something. Which is okay. As long as it makes it better. There might be one or two more of my poems that they may want to use.

Gabriel calls out from the kitchen.

Ric, I will need you in here to assist with the final touches! Everyone else is on red alert! Everyone else do your thing! Isabelle. Isaac. Get the plates out! Em. Get the glasses out! Matt. Get the silverware out! Keli. Gene. Bring out the sides and such! Olivia. Akiva. More wine! Let's move!

I feel the need to point out the obvious.

Ah... Gabriel. You and Ric have already set the table. Plates are out. Glasses are out. And the silverware is out.

And what about napkins?

Napkins are out.

Well, then someone light some damn candles and let's get dinner going. Still waiting for someone to help with the sides!

Keli and Gene move towards the kitchen.

We're on it.

Gene turns to Keli before they reach the kitchen.

When we host next, let's not be like this.

Chapter 37
JUST TWO STRANGERS

Given that the gathering at our house turned out to be a lovely, enjoyable evening, I thought the atmosphere in the studio might now be a little lighter. There is still this air of apprehension. Laurie and I have delved back into working on polishing up some lyrics so they can go ahead and record.

Granted, it's all been a little unsettling. Laurie and I working together again. Our daughters dating. Our spouses enjoying each other's company. Me enjoying her husband's company. Laurie seems to enjoy Isa's company.

The dynamic is, indeed, different when we are around the others. Our lunch with both couples and the kids went fine. It actually didn't end in disaster. Our dinner with everyone also went well. It actually was fun. Perhaps it's when it's just the two of us that...

Did you finish looking at the wording changes we need?

Laurie's question brings me back to the task. My thoughts had drifted away for a few moments. I glance up at Laurie from my usual spot on the floor.

Yes. I'm almost done with coming up with just the right rewording to make them work better.

Laurie just responds to this with a simple nod. She puts down whatever she was working on and flips through the poems on the table. After pulling one in particular out, she looks up. She has that pensive look in her eyes again. She brushes her hair away from her face and tucks it behind her ear.

There was something I was going to ask you a few days ago.

Is this the conversation we were about to have when Devon interrupted us?

Laurie responds again with just a simple nod.

This album is very important to me. I want to be able to focus all my attention on the album and get this out of the space that it's taking up in my head. And, I figure we have to have this discussion at some point.

She, again, holds the poem so I can see which one it is.

Is this one about me?

I consider my options. I could, as Gen would say, just answer the damn question. Which might lead to more questions. Or it might not. The Laurie I once knew would be satisfied with a blunt, one-word yes or no and that would be the end of it. This Laurie might have more questions. Or I could take the opportune moment to keep a working relationship that is productive and jovial, sidestep the question with a flippant remark, and just keep working. Laurie did say that she knows we have to have this discussion at some point. We both still need to tread lightly. I make my choice. I make a feeble attempt to make my response sound light-hearted and nonconfrontational.

Are you so self-centered, so self-absorbed that you think

everything I wrote is about you? I was involved with other women, you know.

So... it is about me.

Of course, it is.

I fumble through a stack of papers and pull out one of the other poems.

This one isn't.

Glancing at the poem in my hand again, I correct my comment.

Oh... wait... yes, it is.

Laurie smiles at this. At least, my comments produced the desired humorous effect. Now we can get back to work.

One other thing...

I guess we're not getting back to work just yet.

...something I've noticed...

Yes?

...about some of these poems...

Yes?

...the ones about the end of our relationship...

Yes?

They seem to have a sense of surrender... no... surrender is not the right word... acceptance... a sense of acceptance.

And what is your point?

I have to ask. Did you ever feel like you wanted us to stay together? Did you ever feel like you wanted me back?

No.

Wow. Now, that was a very quick answer. Didn't have to think about that one at all, did you?

I felt I deserved better. I needed to be loved the way I felt I deserved to be loved. You were unable to do that. You came up with this "I think we should see other people" thing. After what I thought we had been to each other, I didn't want to be just some other guy you were… just also seeing.

Laurie and I look into each other's eyes wondering if there is anything more to say about this. I find that I have another comment to add.

Ultimately, you were far smarter than I about ending the relationship. Things would have eventually ended anyway. Given who we both turned out to be—the kind of people we became—things never would have worked out between us. It was nice for a while, given who we were at that time in our lives. You were right to have ended it when you did… not in the way that you ended it… but… well, there it is.

Interestingly, Laurie has not broken eye contact with me during this. She starts to say something. She seems to change her mind about what she was about to say and takes a deep breath.

Okay. Well, I did ask.

That you did.

We both shift our attention back to the papers in front of us to fidget with various options for the needed changes in my poems to fit the music still playing in the workroom. The instrumental track has been put on a continuous loop so we can try out changes in wording. I am about to suggest we rotate to another piece of music. I like working on several different things at the same time. Laurie likes to get each song done and then move on to another. I acquiesce to her way of doing things. This is, after all, her gig.

Again, I glance up to just a pair of eyes hovering above a sheet of paper. That look is still there. I wait patiently for Laurie to let the thought in her head emerge. It seems that I will need to coax it a little.

Let's just do this. It's still there in your head. Just ask.

Laurie says nothing. She places the paper in front of her off to the side. She places the pad she has been using to make notes off to the side. She takes the copies of my poems that are strewn around the table and places them in neat piles... off to the side. She clicks her pen closed and places it... off to the side. She sits up in her chair. She folds her hands in front of her. She clears her throat.

Did you listen to my album?

I place the sheet of paper in front of me off to the side. I place the pad I've been using to make notes off to the side. I click my pen closed and place it... off to the side. I go to place the poems I have around me in neat piles. They are already in neat piles. I sit up straighter. I fold my hands in front of me. I clear my throat.

Yes. I did.

Aren't you curious if any of the songs are about you?

No.

Wow. Another very quick answer.

I guess I didn't think that our relationship was that...

I should be very careful with what I say here.

...consequential to you. Not enough to write a song about. I never thought that I was anything more to you than a college fling. You do have some songs about the ending of relationships on the album. But I didn't hear anything that I felt related directly to me. And I wasn't going to presume anything.

Laurie slowly repeats some of my own words back to me as she processes that thought.

"I never thought that I was anything more to you than a college fling." You never thought that you were anything more to me than a college fling? Never?

Not afterwards. If I ever meant anything substantial to you, you wouldn't have ended things the way you did. It felt like you had this uncomfortable task to do—getting me out of your life—like taking out the garbage. And, once it was done, you wiped your hands of it and went happily on your way.

There is a momentary, very thick, uncomfortable silence in the room... from us, that is. The instrumental track is still playing. There are some voices from the control room vaguely dripping in. There is some clattering from the break room sliding over. Laurie breaks eye contact with me.

I really don't know how to respond to that right now. Or if I should... right now.

Then don't respond to that right now. Let it go... for now. Or just let it go completely.

We both look down at the papers around us. We both look up at each other waiting to see if one of us has anything more to say. Then we both look back down at our work. Laurie reaches for the lyric page she was working on and makes a tentative move to continue working on it. I pick up the stuff I was working on and reach for my pen. Laurie and I look over at each other another time to check in. I see, in her eyes, that this is all far from over. It seems we both just need a reset.

The clock on the wall changes its numbers a few times. Body language. Facial expressions. Furtive glances. Neither of us is really concentrating very much on what we are doing. I do manage to make a few of the changes to the lyrics and need Laurie to check them. I rise from my position on the floor and place the page I've been working on in front of her. She looks at it.

What happened?

I changed the wording to match the cadence.

Listen to you, using the lingo.

I pay attention. And I know what the word cadence means.

I didn't mean that, though. What happened between us? I mean, what really happened? You see what I did there. I didn't let it go.

Pause.

Oh. We're going to continue that conversation, are we? What happened? The relationship ended.

I know that. I was there, you know.

Then what's the real question?

There is a pause. And then there is a sigh.

What... happened?

Ah... that question. I believe you would know the answer to that question better than I. You were the one who ended it.

We're just going around in circles here. I mean what happened with you.

Okay. If you're really ready for me to go there...

Pause and deep breath while I gather my thoughts on this delicate subject.

Here's my perception of things. In your world, you became dissatisfied with our relationship—dissatisfied with us—dissatisfied with me—you felt it—you thought about it— you pondered it—you reflected on it—you decided you had to do something about it—you decided what to do about it— you planned how to end it—you ended it—and you walked away from it. In your head, you had already processed it and dealt with it and moved on before it ever even happened to me.

A brief pause to let Laurie process that.

In my world, I walked into your house, a man fully and totally in love with you—with a ring in my pocket—only to be greeted by you saying, "I think we should see other people." My entire world crashed in a single moment. In seven words.

Pause.

I never thought about it that way before.

How could you?

Are you saying… do you mean to… are you accusing me of being thoughtless about it?

I am not saying that… exactly, and I am not accusing you of anything. I am saying that we each experienced the breakup in our own way. Besides, what would be the point of delving further? We've been working together. Getting along fine. We are actually having a personal, thoughtful conversation. Why ruin that?

Well, then let me ask about your letter to Maggie. Was that just you trying to hurt me? A vindictive thing? To get back at me for hurting you?

Again, I don't see the point of dealing with that—for now, at least. We are only just at the point of really speaking to each other again.

Just trying to get answers to some lingering questions. Just trying to deal with the awkwardness of it all.

Why is this so awkward? We're both happily married. I'm sorry, I didn't mean to presume. You are happily married, aren't you?

Yes! Of course! Very!

As am I. Well, there it is. So, this doesn't need to be awkward. I don't even like you anymore.

Well, if that doesn't make this whole thing thoroughly awkward…

I mean, I don't know you anymore… I mean… I don't know the you who you are now. At least, not enough to like or dislike you.

Maybe that's why it is so awkward. We're basically two

strangers trying to have an intimate conversation about something that happened in the past... to two other people.

Maggie said something like that during a conversation I was having with her.

You talked to Maggie about us?

Let it go... for now. But there is a great idea in there somewhere for some lyrics for another song. Except for the "basically." It's such a non-musical word. Let's change that to, we're only two strangers trying to have... no, change that to, just two strangers... write that down.

Said with a slight, light touch of humor—

Don't tell me what to do. And you're the lyricist on this. You write that down.

With a slight smile—

Fine. I'll write it down. Let's get back to work and finish this song. Don't think we should spend any longer with each other than we absolutely need to.

At least we can agree on that.

A sarcastic response to Laurie's last comment begins to make its way to my mouth. My brain opts to fight that impulse and stay silent. Laurie chooses to not stay silent.

No. Let's not get back to work, just yet. Let's finish this now. Let's talk about this thing we haven't said yet. Alright, let's just get this out there. I hurt you. Doesn't that bother you?

No. Not really.

Why not?

It did, of course, obviously...

I gesture to my poems on the table.

...at the time. Not anymore. And you didn't hurt me. That other Laurie hurt that other Isaac.

Now you're just screwing around with semantics.

Indeed, I am. It puts things in perspective.

Why doesn't it bother you?

Anymore.

Why doesn't it bother you... anymore?

First of all, it happened over thirty years ago. More importantly, I was not supposed to end up with you. You were not supposed to end up with me. I was supposed to end up with Isa. You were supposed to end up with Paul. What happened between the two of us just made sure that other events in our lives happened the way that they were meant to. I love how things worked out. I can't be upset about something that ultimately set us both on our right paths.

That is so highly evolved of you.

It's the life lesson you, indirectly, taught me by breaking up with me. Thank you.

You're welcome... I guess. But, you know, technically, I didn't break up with you. I only said we should see other people and you took it upon yourself to...

The look I am now giving Laurie stops her from finishing that thought.

Okay, okay... point taken.

Silence. Laurie is flipping through the various pages of my poems. She appears to find the one she is looking for and places it on top of the pile.

In *Beautiful Storm*, you refer to me as a mistake. You still feel that way?

What makes you think that one was about you?

You still want to play it that way?

Okay, fine.

You write a poem about someone else that you refer to as a songbird?

I said fine.

So, was I a mistake to you?

No. I eventually embraced the idea that I needed to go through you to get to who I became. That poem... well, that was the way I was feeling at the time.

Another silence from us permeates the room. We glance around, unsure of what our next move is. It's as if we were both expecting some dramatic manifestation of a sign or signal that our worlds were somehow changed... somehow now different. That some colossal purge had occurred. Some trumpets or fanfare. There's nothing but the silence. That is, except for the instrumental track still playing in the background... until Laurie speaks up.

Are we done?

Not quite. This is good. This is like flushing this all out one last time.

That's an interesting choice of imagery.

There are just so many things we didn't say to each other when we should have. Here's a rhetorical question...

You do not want an answer to it?

I do not. Your answer would not make any difference to me in any way whatsoever anyway.

Okay... go ahead.

If, after you said you thought we should see other people...

Yes?

Instead of me asking if you wanted me to leave...

Yes?

If I hadn't been dealing with the shock of you telling me you wanted us to see other people when I was about to ask you to marry me...

Yes?

What if we had discussed what was bothering you

instead of me just shutting down? What if I had asked you what does that make our relationship now? I don't mean now... I mean back then. I don't want an answer, but you should think about what your response might have been.

But you don't want an answer.

Any answer, for me, would be meaningless.

So, why am I supposed to think about this?

It's something you should grapple with in your head. Things might have ended more amicably... more pleasantly... between us. We might have even remained friends. It might help us with figuring out whatever our relationship is turning into now. There might be an idea for another song in there to finish the album out. It is, after all, kind of turning into a concept album about relationships.

Then there's a pause. Laurie seems to have several thoughts being sorted out in her head. The first few seem troubling to her. The next few seem a little more pleasant to her. I see in her eyes she has something to say to me.

So, are we okay?

We both smile as that idea meanders through both our heads.

Yes. We're good. What was that phrase you were supposed to write down?

Just two strangers. And it was you who was supposed to write it down.

Chapter 38
BEHIND YOUR EYES

Night falls quietly
Allowing the illumination
From behind your eyes
To spill out
And drip down as glistening drops
Splashing over silken skin
Running down
Forming a deep pool in which to rest
In sleep and reams in each other's hearts
I wake at dawn and watch
As the sun is noiselessly lured
In through our window
And kisses you lightly on the eyes
And beckons me to do the same
Which brings a smile
From your lips
For us to share.

Chapter 39
TIME FOR REFLECTION

I send *Behind Your Eyes* off to the publisher. They probably already have the song lyric version from Laurie since she's done with that one. I realize that my not having worked on the collection of poems for a while was not, as I had said last night, because I was working in the studio so much. Well, in a way, it was.

There's been another poem swirling around in my head. Just some scattered lines so far. About Isa.

My hesitation about moving forward on the poems for the book was because I was waiting for these new thoughts about Isa to form a little more. I needed to give them some space before focusing any more of my attention on the book. A book with poems, mostly, about other women... mostly Laurie.

Isa said something last night that resonated with me. About us appreciating each other more at this point in our relationship. Those other poems were taking up space in my head. Now these other thoughts, about Isa, need their space. So, I write *Dive*. And that'll be another one for my book of poetry.

Chapter 40
DIVE

I dip my hands
Into the depths of you
And drink deep

You dip your hands
Into my soul
And splash your face

Merge together
Meld together
We both dive in
And we are one

I dive into you
and I'm alive again
with you

These days
We never want to end
These nights

Buddy Lee Walter

I can't get enough of you

I need to be the smile
That comes to your lips in your sleep
I need to be the fire
That warms you in the cold of night
I need to be the umbrella
That shelters you in the rain that falls
I need to be your shade
In the glaring light of doubt
I need to be your temptation
I need to be what you need me to be

You are my power, my passion,
My grace, my muse

I dive into you
And I'm alive again
With you

Take me to that place
Where the world slows down
And it's only you and me

Fingers intertwined
Lives intertwined
Souls intertwined

I dive into you
And I'm alive again
With you

Chapter 41
ARE YOU SURE?

S o... Laurie, are you saying that you don't want the album to have any detailed liner notes?

This morning has been a flurry of activity in the studio. I have basically just sat out of the way—in the corner—on the floor—with my copy of the *Tao Te Ching*—while all these things were swirling around me. Finishing up this. Completing that. Rerecording a drum part. Remixing a bass part. I was asked to be there to make sure I was okay with a few minor alterations to some lyrics. For the past few minutes, Laurie and I have been sitting across from each other at the workroom table looking over a rough draft of the liner notes. Devon is sitting at the other end of the table working on something of his own.

No, Isaac. What I am saying is that the liner notes for the album are going to be just the names of the musicians, who is playing what instrument on which track, and a few general thoughts. Me as composer. You as lyricist.

What about specific comments about the songs?

I don't like that idea. I believe a song should simply be

presented without any explanation. The songs should stand by themselves without us leading the listener to any specific interpretation. Let the songs resonate with them however they do.

The writer in me wants to explain.

But the listener should embrace the song in whatever way they want to. When you're in a museum you don't get a commentary from the artist about what the painting is about.

I see your point. But I have all these thoughts in my head about what was going on in my head when I wrote these pieces.

Keep them in your head. Let the listener react to the songs in their own way. When you publish a book, you don't add an addendum explaining the book or add commentary along the way. You let the reader discover their own path in.

But I do write a preface with some thoughts.

And we are going to have that. Just not specific comments about the meaning behind each song.

I pause to reflect for a moment. Laurie studies the look on my face.

Are you still not sure what I mean?

No. I get it. I was just thinking... our first fight?

This is not a fight.

First argument?

Not really. Just two different points of view. But mine is the right one.

I do get it. You're right. And I do still think of this as your thing. It's your album. I've just been along for the ride.

Laurie leans forward and sorts through several pieces of paper in front of her. She pulls out two, sets them on top of the pile. She then leans back in her chair. She glances up at the clock on the wall.

About that. Here's what I've been thinking.

And, trust me, I've put a lot of thought into this.

Go on.

And the others agree...

Who are these others?

Devon. The other musicians.

The studio guys. And Derek.

Go on.

I'm pulling out the few songs that I had already written, on my own, from the album. We've already decided to use them for a third album. The songs that I wrote on my own don't really fit, conceptually or thematically or stylistically, with the ones we've done together.

Again, this is your album. Why are you telling me this?

But it is not my album anymore. It hasn't been for a while. It's our album. We've been collaborating. It's my music but the lyrics are mostly yours. This album would be just the songs we've worked on together. Just the ones with your lyrics.

And that's enough pieces to use?

Well, that's the thing.

Laurie takes the pieces of papers from the top of the pile and places them between us.

I've taken the liberty of using another one of your poems, *Captured Angel*. I'd already written music for it. We've actually already recorded it. I do hope you're okay with that. I know I should have spoken to you about it first. But I got inspired and excited by this idea. We were in the studio finishing up recording another piece. I wanted to try out what I'd come up with about *Captured Angel*. As an experiment. To see if it would work. It did. I'd like you to listen to it later to get your approval. And there were these others. She gestures to the several pieces of paper in front of her.

I was having a little bit of difficulty deciding which ones to use. So, I decided to use *Vigil* and *Primal Poem* as well.

Laurie glances up at the clock again and then looks back at me.

Your percentage would, of course, increase.

I study Laurie's face for a moment.

This is an incredibly courageous thing for you to do.

The quality of this album is very important to me.

I don't have any problem with any of this.

It's Laurie's turn to study my face for a moment.

Well, okay then. Fine.

But I do think we should agree that, as interesting as this has been, there would be no intention of us continuing to collaborate after we are done here.

Agreed. And agreed that it has been interesting.

I just have other things to get back to. Some other dragons to slay.

As do I. And we'll still be around each other a little bit because of Rowena and Genevieve's relationship. And I would like it... if you would like to... if you would show up in the studio every so often when I'm working on the next album. You've been pleasant company. And Devon would miss you too much.

Devon looks up from his work.

You are, ever so much, welcome here. Your presence here... well, it's like when Billy Preston was in the studio with the Beatles. Everyone is on their proper behavior.

Devon promptly goes back to his task. Laurie glances up at the clock for a third time.

At some point we should have a discussion regarding

your definition of pleasant company. You keep checking the time. Is there a problem?

No. Not at all. Derek told me he was going to stop by the studio. He has another idea to share with us.

Laurie changes the subject before I have a chance to respond to this.

I wanted to ask you something else.

Go ahead and ask.

It's about that not knowing what happened in our lives after college thing.

Okay.

Weren't you ever curious enough to do a Facebook snoop? I was. I did.

I smile at this.

Back when you joined the alumni group page, I did snoop. I saw that you changed your last name to a stage name. But that was the name that showed up when you joined the group. I looked at your page. I saw that you were married. You looked happy. I was pleased. That was enough for me. But I made the decision, once our relationship was over, to not revisit that episode in my life. If you remember, after the breakup, I even sent you that photo of us. I believe that was the only photo of us together. I know it was the only one of us together that I had. Well, other than the photos from one of the dances we choreographed together. I let go of everything.

It is at this very moment that we are distracted by the door to the studio opening. Derek enters. He looks around. He sees us in the workroom. He smiles and waves. Devon waves him in. He heads for the door to the workroom.

I look at Laurie.

Derek has another idea? I'm intrigued. Do you know what this is about?

Laurie does not answer this question. Derek has entered the room and grandly takes a seat at the table.

I hear things have been going great and the album is just about done. Good. Good to hear that. I believe this is right on our original time frame. You both are looking good. Here's my thought.

Derek focuses his attention on me.

I've been involved in these discussions about Laurie taking the songs she wrote by herself and dumping them into a third album. Cool. So, now this album is basically musically hers. Basically, lyrically yours. Yes, I know you've been collaborating with each other on both of those things a little. I also thought about the fact that your lyrics were written very long ago. Not written specifically for an album. I think it would be fantastic if you had one song on the album that the two of you write together. To bring the whole thing full circle. I mean, actually do a real collaboration.

There is quiet in the room. Laurie, Derek, and Devon wait for me to respond. I'm thinking.

Wow. This is just like the reaction I got at the reunion when I suggested the two of you working together. This is not that difficult. The album is songs with her music and your lyrics. Write one piece together where you, Isaac, are involved in working with Laurie on the music and Laurie is involved in working with you on writing the lyrics. She was writing her own lyrics before you joined in on this.

I just know that this is not going to come out just the way I mean it, but I try to express my thoughts as well as I can.

The ability to do it is not really the issue here. Laurie is a wonderful lyric writer in her own right. I know enough about composition and melody to help write the music.

So?

We have been collaborating. But we've been just piecing things together. We haven't been creating something totally new. Some music she already had. Some poems I already had. Fidget with them a little bit. Change this. Move that. What you're asking is…

I pause and turn to Laurie.

You knew about this?

Yes. Derek and I and the others had discussed it.

And you thought this was a good idea?

Yes. I liked the idea. I thought that a piece completely written by both of us—not just music by me and lyrics by you—would be a great way to finish an album with songs about relationships.

I turn my attention back to Derek.

What you're asking is… instead of us… Laurie and I… just adapting my poems into song lyrics… that we write a song together. We've been working together… I would say we've been working well together.

Laurie adds to my comment.

We have been working well together. We have almost an entire album of material. I feel… we all feel that we need one more song to pull the entire thing together. And that song should be something of a tighter, closer, collaboration.

You see, that's the point right there. Something of a tighter, closer collaboration. We've been working together but there has still been this boundary between us. Writing something new together opens up that boundary. Especially if it's about us. I just don't know if I am comfortable with that.

Well, I don't want you to feel uncomfortable with any of this.

Perhaps I just need to get used to the idea. Give me some time to process this.

Both Devon and Derek have the same question and speak almost at the same time.

How much time?

Laurie intervenes.

Let Isaac do what he needs to do. Meanwhile, we can continue planning the album launch party.

Devon interjects.

How can we plan an album launch if...?

His comment is interrupted by a look from Laurie. I attempt to allay their concerns.

I know. I know. I understand. But all of you have been thinking about this, pondering it, planning it and discussing it. This is a new idea... a surprise... to me.

I make eye contact with Laurie.

Only this time I don't have a ring in my pocket.

Laurie breaks eye contact with me.

Again, both Devon and Derek have the same question and speak almost at the same time.

What?

Laurie glances at the others.

I know what he means.

I look at Devon and Derek. Their faces express consternation. I look over at Laurie. Her face expresses thoughtfulness. I appreciate that.

I'm in.

Are you sure?

You want me to agree to this and then ask me if I'm sure when I do?

Fair enough. Okay. Good. I'm pleased.

I just needed a few moments to think this through.

There are ramifications to this that we need to be cognizant of.

Devon again interjects.

I think you're smart enough to deal with that. After all, you're someone who uses words like ramification and cognizant. You'll be fine.

The slightest thread of doubt emerges from the depths. I lock eyes with Laurie.

Will we?

Chapter 42
CAPTURED ANGEL

Try, though you may
To capture the notes of a dream
Floating on a sigh,
They elude your grasp.
You may, however,
Touch them gently with your hopes.
Now
Is the only time we ever have,
Or ever had
Or ever will.
A moment lingers not long in our lives,
Pausing ever so briefly on our souls,
Then disappearing into the all there is –
Vanishing into the way or why not –
Vaporizing into the ever after –
Leaving behind a mere reflection
In the labyrinth of my mind
Of a night–a moment under the stars,
Of a kiss–sweet and tender,

In These Little Moments

Of a melody–that caresses my ear,
Of an angel–held in my thoughts.
Try, though you may,
To capture the notes of a dream...

Chapter 43
OH, SO NOW IT'S "WE"

Settling in to do some work on my book of poetry, ready for final checking so it's prepared for publication. I get some music going. This time it's some funk. Preparing the poems *Captured Angel*, *Vigil*, and *Primal Poem* for the book. I am working on the changes that were made to the poems in the studio. Laurie has an astounding ability to take something, originally written in poetic form, pull out the essence of it, and add or change what is needed to make it work as a song. She sees things in them that I would not have.

As usual, I keep Facebook open and solitaire nearby to take a momentary break from the work every so often. This morning, Facebook has been unusually quiet. That is, until...

Hi, Isaac! How are things going? Am I interrupting anything?

It's a message from Courtney. I respond.

An interruption from you is always a welcome one.

It just seems like I'm always interrupting.

I'm just often doing something around the times you

usually message me. I always have several projects going at the same time. You know what? I'll call you the next time I'm just taking some down time.

Working on another book?

That and a few other things.

Well, I hope things are going well.

Things are going nicely. I've just been finishing up editing some more pages for my poetry book.

I continue checking my notes on the changes to the poems while I wait for Courtney's next message.

Cool. Looking forward to it coming out! Still planning on releasing it the same time as the album?

Yes. And we will invite you to the release party when we decide when it will be. You were, after all, there when this whole thing began.

I reflect, for a moment, on the fact that I used the word *we* instead of *I*.

That would be exciting! Have you invited any of the others?

Since this collaboration was Derek's idea, he and Amelia will be there. And, yes, a few of the others that were around when we were discussing this at the reunion.

So, what are you doing with the poems? Thought they were already written?

The poems, as I originally wrote them, were already part of the collection. Now I just need to also add the way they will appear as song lyrics on the album with the changes we've been making.

Oh, okay. I know I said I would keep my mouth shut about this… but how is everything between you and Laurie? You know… in the studio… and all that? Are the two of you okay?

There's that question again.

I think that some people around us have been more concerned about this than we are.

What do you mean?

We're fine. It seems that some other people around us are expecting this to be a problem. It isn't. We're just working together. Well, not just working together. Our daughters are dating. So, we've been spending some time together.

Your daughter? And Laurie's daughter? Wow.

And we went out to lunch with Isa and Paul and the kids. Isa and I also had them over to our house for dinner a little while ago. So, we're all getting along just fine. No problems. Yet, people keep asking that question.

Sorry. I get it. I'll stop asking.

It's not just you. But thank you.

At least it'll be one less person asking about it.

At least there's that.

Can I ask then...

Here we go.

...how are Isa and Paul with all this?

Isa is supportive of all this. She understands that Laurie and I have a working relationship. And that none of this has any effect on our marriage. I would actually say that—and I hope this doesn't come out mean in any way—being around Laurie, if anything, has just made me appreciate my wife even more.

And Paul?

I have no idea what is going on in Paul's head. He seems to be okay with it.

Okay then. I guess I'll see you all at the launch party. Get back to your work.

I do so.

Chapter 44
VIGIL

Tonight
the wind is howling
down a time-beaten,
deserted shore.
Sand is tossed around
the powerful statues
of rock
that jut out against
an open sea.
A moon hangs softly
in a tortured sky
with a deep blue, fluorescent glow,
and the shadows that are cast
on the sand
dance as the clouds tease the moon.
All is deathly still
tonight
except for the wind and the waves
crashing against the towering cliffs
that beckon lost souls to pass here.

Buddy Lee Walter

One such soul walks the sands this night.
Not much more than a breeze himself,
this lone figure rides the winds.
He glances around him,
momentarily noticing the strange shapes
the rocks become
in the lighting set for this scene.
He does not dwell on the thought for long.
The rocks, the waves, the sand, and moon
are all too familiar to him,
as he has walked this haven
for a time that spans many lifetimes.
He lifts his eyes toward the endless sea
and whispers a woman's name.
The wind gently tugs at his hair.
The sounds of the wind and sea are joined
by a soft, slow, silent cry
tonight.

Chapter 45
LIVES INTERTWINE

The evening is winding down nicely. There are the remains of our chicken and steak dinner scattered about the living room. It has been Keli and Gene's turn to host, and Gene just bought this new barbecue. We took the opportunity to enjoy our dinner outside on the patio. As the sun disappeared, we moved back inside the house.

Everyone has been quite busy over the last few weeks, so we've all enjoyed an evening to just relax a bit. Rick has been telling us about some upgrades he's having done in his restaurant kitchen. Gabriel has just completed editing a new film. Emma is starting some new meditation programs at her wellness center. We've been discussing the various projects that the others have been working on. Isa sits on the couch next to Olivia. I sit on the floor between them with my arm draped over Isa's legs. Olivia has been telling Isa about the work she's been doing, as a violinist, on an album. She's been working with a jazz group that wanted violin on some of their album's tracks. She's enjoying venturing away from the usual classical pieces she's been playing with the orchestra.

The scents of the barbecue mingle with the lilacs from outside and drift in. Those lilacs were from cuttings Isa and I gave them from ours. Nice to see—and smell—the flowers doing well.

Olivia shifts her wine glass to her other hand and places her hand on my shoulder.

So, Isaac, have you been in the studio lately?

I have. The album is just about done. We're working on writing one more song. Then it just needs to be recorded. The album should be done after that and ready for release. And you're all invited to the album and poetry book launch party. I will let you know when the date is finalized.

There are a variety of responses, such as, "That sounds great"... "Looking forward to that"... "Groovy."

And we'll get to meet this Laurie?

She'll be there, of course.

Matt leans forward in his chair across from us.

And will you be continuing working at all in the world of music?

I take a sip from my wine glass.

I don't think so. This whole thing has been an incredible learning experience. I've enjoyed being part of what goes on in a recording studio. I love music. I've often thought of myself having the soul of a musician. Just not the skill. I'll likely stay in touch with Devon, this album producer I became friends with. I just don't see myself continuing to work in that environment. After this thing is done, I want to get back to working on my book.

There's a momentary silence. It's as if the others are waiting for me to say something else. I have nothing else to add to the conversation. Akiva realizes that no one else is going to ask the question the rest of them have.

And what about Laurie?

What about her?

What about your relationship with her?

Neither of us see the two of us working together on another album, if that is what you're asking. We will still be around each other. Our lives will still intertwine. At least, as long as our daughters are dating.

Isa leans forward to place her wine glass on the table in front of us.

Well, that's going to continue to be a thing. Rowena is a delightful young lady. And they're good for each other. They're happy together. Laurie comes as part of that package, I guess.

Keli rises and begins gathering up a few of the plates and silverware.

And you're saying that works for everyone?

Isa also rises to help clean up.

It seems to. Gene and I used to date, and we've made that work. We've already spent some time together with Laurie and her husband, Paul. He's interesting. Paul and I had a great conversation about interior design. Isaac and he had a good time discussing The Beatles and fencing when we had them to our house for dinner. I'm not saying we're all going to end up great friends. But, for the sake of the girls' relationship, we have to make this work. So, we will.

Everyone seems to accept that. The rest of us join in cleaning up and putting things away as the sound of crickets joins in with the music.

Chapter 46
PRIMAL POEM

Sing woman
sing your song of enticement
like a snake, coiled and ready to strike
like a siren, luring sailors to their death.
Go on
draw him close to you
but not close enough for you to lose yourself
but close enough for your ego's pleasure.
Primal screams echo inside him
primal passions surge.
The pain is silent to all ears, except his own
but it shines through his eyes like beacons in the night
warning all to stay far away
warning all of the pain inside
of the agony
of a touch
that is no more
than a touch.
Only she dares to come near

and she will not stay for long
just long enough to drain him of hope.
Dream woman
dream your dream of dreams.

Chapter 47
WE'VE BEEN HERE BEFORE

Laurie and I have been sitting at the workroom table for—I glance up at the clock—fourteen minutes. It seems much longer. During those interminable fourteen minutes, there have been several times when I've had a thought, started to say something, but changed my mind and kept silent. There have been several intakes of breath from Laurie, as if she is about to speak. These have been followed by a sigh and silence.

Laurie reaches for her cup of coffee on the table. She takes a drink from her coffee mug. I have been in the habit of bringing my own coffee in a travel mug which also sits on the table. I take a drink from it.

Devon had come into the room earlier to ask if his presence would make this easier or harder. Laurie and I both shrugged. He left the room. I offer an idea to at least get us started.

We could... what if we both—on our own—just start writing... you know, brainstorming things? And then we compare notes. Pick out ideas that work together?

The look that I am getting from Laurie suggests that this is not going to happen that way.

Okay, never mind. I realize that that's not the point of this.

Laurie looks down. There is a thought floating around in her head. She looks up at me. She brushes back her hair from over her face and tucks it behind her ears.

Let's just get out of here.

And go where?

I don't know. Let's just point ourselves in a direction and walk. Maybe we just need to get out of the workroom. Everything we've done in here has been my music and your lyrics. A change of locale might be what we need.

That's a good idea. Let's go.

I gather up a pad and pen. After informing Devon of our plans, we exit the studio. Laurie, standing on my right, makes a move to go left. We collide into each other. Pad and pen end up on the sidewalk. Once I've retrieved these items, I gesture the way that Laurie was intending to go, and we go.

As we walk, we attempt to engage in discussion about this song. I offer an idea.

Perhaps starting with the lyrics isn't the best place to begin. Perhaps we need to deal with the music first.

Laurie considers this.

I don't think so. We both write words. I'm the one that has been writing music. If we start that way, I'm concerned the music might be mostly coming from me. I want to be careful not to take the lead on the music. I think it will work better if we write the lyrics. Then you and I, together, can come up with the melody. That would make it more ours. I can do what I need to with it from there.

Good point.

I have a recollection of saying, "That's not the point of this," back at the studio. The word *point* has stuck in my head. We walk some more.

Finally, I think I have a bit of a thought about, at least, where to begin.

Point of view.

What?

Let's start with point of view. First person or third person?

Well, most songs are better in first person. It makes it more personal.

We stop walking, momentarily, as I consider this.

But then, whose point of view? Yours or mine?

We begin walking again. Laurie tries to grapple with that question.

If we are writing the song together, and it's about us... should it be "we" or "they"?

So... third person, but whether it's subjective or objective?

We walk some more. Getting out of the studio seems to have been a great idea. At least we've started doing something. I guess anything is better than sitting at the worktable just waiting for something to happen.

Laurie takes a deep breath and brushes her hair back from her face, tucking it behind her ears. A sign that there are thoughts in her head she is in the midst of dealing with. This could either be good or bad.

We're doing it again, you know.

I glance over at Laurie, waiting for her to finish that thought.

We're not saying the thing that really needs to be said. We did that. We do that. Too much.

Go on.

I concentrate on the rhythm of our walking as I let Laurie put the rest of her thoughts together.

We're talking about first person, third person, subjective, objective. We're not talking about what the song is about.

We both stop walking as this idea sinks in. I offer my opinion.

A safety valve, perhaps. Begin with the basic stuff. Begin with the easy answers. Begin with the stuff without the high emotional content.

Laurie looks over my shoulder.

An early lunch?

I glance in the direction Laurie is looking. I see the entrance to the courtyard that leads to the restaurant where we all had lunch before. We head that way.

We enter the restaurant. We ask if Tonya is working today. She is. We ask for a table with her. As the hostess takes us over to a table in Tonya's section, I take notice of the song playing in the restaurant. My mind drifts back to a memory I have of a night out roller-skating with Laurie to this song. I am contemplating whether to share this memory of our past with Laurie or not as I pull out a chair for Laurie to sit, move to my side of the table, and put the writing pad and pen down. As I sit down, Tonya approaches with two glasses of water which she places on our table along with menus. Laurie and I both look up at her. There is no sign of recognition in Tonya's eyes. Neither of us says anything.

Tonya greets us with a warm welcome. She asks if we've been here before. Laurie tells her that we have. Tonya responds, "Welcome back," and that she will give us a few minutes to look at the menu and come back shortly.

Laurie and I both take a look at our menus. I glance up over the top of my menu and see Laurie's eyes just over the top of hers. She has an expectant look in her eyes. There's a moment more of silence before I ask the question.

What are you thinking?

You were about to say something as we sat down. You changed your mind?

I place my menu down. She does the same with hers.

This song...

I wait for Laurie to listen and realize what song is playing before continuing.

...was playing when you and I were out roller skating. I actually asked the DJ to play it. For us.

You have a good memory.

The song triggered that memory. I was wondering whether I should bring it up or not.

No harm in sharing a memory from our past. Maybe that would help us with writing the song.

We both pick up our menus and continue to look at them. We aren't particularly hungry. We just really wanted a change of view from the studio. We decide to order two appetizers to share and sit here and work on the song lyrics. Tonya swings by and cheerfully takes our order and scurries off.

I place the writing pad in front of me and begin to make some notes.

So, the song. Third person. Subjective—we. Or objective—they. Or are we not starting there now? Are we starting with what the song is about?

I think we should start with what the song is about.

What is it about?

What?

This was your idea. You. And Derek. And Devon. And the musicians. And the studio guys. My contribution was poems that I wrote that we turned into song lyrics. I thought that was it. And now, you're asking me... asking us... to say something more. What more is there to say?

Okay. I understand now. Let's start over. Let's start from the beginning.

The beginning of what?

Laurie pauses while she considers her response to this.

I don't know. The songs on the album are about us. They're based on things you wrote—about us—while we were involved—and about us—after the breakup.

Another pause while we contemplate what all this means. I place the pad and pen off to the side.

What do you want to say—to me—about us?

Laurie locks eyes with me. Her brow furrows slightly.

I don't know.

What do you want me to say—to you—about us?

I don't know.

You see the problem?

I do.

Yet another pause. After a few moments I offer a suggestion.

Let's just brainstorm a bit. Let's try to objectify this whole thing. There was this couple. They met in college and dated. They worked on performances together. They moved in together. Fast forward. Things ended. Things ended badly. They don't speak to each other or think about each other for almost forty years. The paths of these two people cross again.

And?

And... I don't know where I was going with that.

It's at this moment that Tonya comes over to our table. She sets down our two appetizers, two empty plates, and some silverware. The three of us exchange some pleasantries. Tonya goes off to another table where people have just been seated and she greets them.

Before we got to the restaurant—outside—I said we're not talking about us.

You said that we were not talking about what the song was about. That's slightly different.

I take one of the plates and place it in front of Laurie. I place the other in front of me. I place a set of silverware next to her plate and one next to mine. I move the appetizers to the middle of the table. I begin to serve Laurie half of each. As she sometimes does, Laurie begins to speak. She changes her mind. She then makes the decision to say it.

What would my husband and your wife say if they saw us here together?

What is the point of the question?

Just wondering if that is a good angle to get us started writing. We're out alone together.

We're not alone. We're sitting in a crowded...

I take a look around the restaurant.

...we're sitting in a semi-empty-lunch-time-crowd restaurant. Are you suggesting this is any different than us sitting in the studio having something to eat while we work? You suggested we take a walk. I agreed. We ended up here. A place we have been before... with both Isa and Paul.

We both take a few bites of our food. I offer another idea.

Here's the situation. After not being in each other's lives for a few decades, we find ourselves involved in a project again. We come to the realization that we don't really know each other at all.

So, is this going to be a "Where do we go from here?" thing? That's not what this last song should be. That doesn't fit in with the rest of the songs on the album.

Okay. This is good. At least we're realizing what we don't want the song to be about.

I write a few notes on the pad.

What did you write?

This last song.

Why?

You just said it. It might be a good title. Or...

I add a few more words to the pad.

...our last song.

Okay. Do you often start with the title?

No. Never. Well, until right now. That's not completely true. I write down these thoughts. Words. Phrases. They just sometimes emerge. They usually end up somewhere in there as part of the piece. Occasionally, they might end up as the title of the poem or the title of a chapter. It depends on how it resonates...

The sound of a clatter of dishes, coming from the kitchen area, distracts us for a moment. We take a few more bites from our food. Laurie takes our conversation in a different direction.

You just said something about us not knowing each other anymore. I do feel... well... I've been reading and studying your poems about me... about our relationship. I do feel I know you a bit after doing that. Maybe that's our starting point for this.

I put down the food that I had in my hand. I wipe my hands with my napkin. I look down to process my thoughts. I look up to lock eyes with Laurie. I lean in.

Don't, for a moment, believe that you know me now because you read some poems I wrote. We knew each other, briefly, over thirty years ago. Deeply—yes—albeit briefly. These are poems I wrote decades ago—poems I wrote from an emotional... gangplank... a place of hurt, pain, and confusion, upon which the light was shut, and the door was closed a long time ago. Poems written from a place that doesn't exist anymore. They don't reveal anything about who I am now. Any more so than if I claimed to know you because I listened to a few songs on your album.

Okay. Fair enough. You threw some nice imagery and stuff in there, though.

Tonya swings past our table. She stops long enough to ask if everything is okay. We nod. She saunters off to another table. Laurie comes up with another thought.

We were together. There are songs about that. Then we weren't together. There are songs about that. And then...

Then what?

So, if it's not a "Where do we go from here?" thing... maybe it's a "Where do we go from then here?" thing.

Then here?

Back then here. Not now here. Back then here. The end of our relationship. We, ultimately, ended up, as you have pointed out, in the relationships we were meant to be in. On the paths we were meant to be on.

That would make this last song a positive, uplifting thing. Good way to end the album.

Exactly. What would the reaction be from the poet in you?

I ponder that thought for a moment.

These things happen... things that happen... events that compartmentalize... sort... your life into before this thing happened and into after this thing happened. Where things will never be the same after this thing. You will be different. There's a "before this thing" you and an "after this thing" you. Signposts. Pointing in the direction you need to go in. Often at a crossroad.

Laurie, I think somewhat unconsciously, puts her hand over mine.

And that doesn't necessarily make it a bad thing... just a thing that happened.

She realizes where her hand is and quickly moves to pick up some food from her plate. I reach for the pad and pen.

What are you writing now?

I'll let you know when I've thought it out more.

We're writing this song together.

Right. Sorry. Just a habit. I wrote *signposts*.

And then, also write down *crossroad*.

I do so. A few other thoughts come to me.

Now what are you writing?

Burning bridges. River runs deep. Ripples in the water. Opposite sides of the shore. Different paths.

Laurie looks up. I can see her running these things through her head. She looks back at me.

Is this how you create? Bits and pieces?

I nod.

Mostly. I get flashes of images. I collect them. Eventually they fall into their place. Like pieces of a puzzle.

Is that just with your poetry? What about your novels?

It's the same way. At least they start out that way. Inspirational insights. With a novel, eventually the characters become fully developed and they sort of tell me where they want to go. They often surprise me with choices that they make. How about you?

It's always different. Sometimes it's the whole idea of the song. What the song is about. Sometimes it's a phrase that comes into my head and I build around that. And I, too, am sometimes surprised about what comes out.

Music first or lyrics first?

Both. It depends on where the inspiration comes from.

At this moment, Tonya strides over to our table.

Can I get you two anything else?

Laurie looks at me. I shake my head.

Just the check, please.

Tonya has a sudden epiphany. She looks at Laurie. She looks at me. She giggles. Her face brightens. She smiles.

Separate checks?

Chapter 48
GHOSTS IN THE MIST

She looked off one way
He looked off the other
He looked at her
She looked away
Seeking answers
to questions
left unasked

Standing on opposite sides
of an ever-widening river
Thinking about
what might have been
Thinking about
what they are leaving behind
on the other side

No more I love you's
[Are you happy now?]
Ghosts in the mist
[Erase the memory of you]

Buddy Lee Walter

Just two strangers
[Is there life after love?]

This river runs deep
but they only
skimmed the surface
And now they just stare
at the ripples
in the water
just fading away

Wind rushes
Lightning strikes
Thunder crashes

No more I love you's
[Are you happy now?]
Ghosts in the mist
[Erase the memory of you]
Just two strangers
[Is there life after love?]

Echoes from the past
swirl around them
whispering all the things
they once said
Echoes of all the things
in their heads
of all the things
they should have said

In the flickering light
of their bridge burning

In These Little Moments

the wind abates
the lightning ebbs
the thunder fades away

No more I love you's
[Are you happy now?]
Ghosts in the mist
[Erase the memory of you]
Just two strangers
[Is there life after love?]

Somewhere out there
beyond the right and the wrong
part of the heart gets lost
on the way
to a better way

The storm drifts away
The dark clouds disappear
A shaft of sunlight pierces through

They leave it all behind
and it takes
a little more time
on the way
to being
strangers again

They can't see it yet
but it's out there
at the end of the road

No more I love you's

Buddy Lee Walter

[They're both happy now]
Ghosts in the mist
[Embrace the memory of you]
Just two strangers
[Finding life after love]

Chapter 49
ANSWERS–OR NOT

Are you happy now? Is that an honest question or a sarcastic question?

After posing this question, Laurie sets the lyric sheet back down on the worktable. She leans forward, with her elbow on the table, and sets her chin on the back of her palm as her fingers dangle. This seemed to be a simple enough question, about one of a few last lyrics I inserted in our song. Asked without animosity. Just curiosity.

Isn't that the splendid thing about song lyrics... about art? You can interpret them in a myriad of ways. That's what makes it interesting.

I'm the one singing the line.

Laurie pauses. She takes a breath before continuing.

It would be nice to know what you are thinking.

You just do your thing. You just sing it like you want to or need to. Let the listener decide if it's honest or sarcastic. Someone once said something like that to me. I believe it was you.

Fine.

You actually don't have to sing it. I would like those

lines that I put in brackets to be sort of just in the background. Like an echo would sound. Even though it's not an echo.

I get it. I do like it.

It doesn't have to be your voice. It could be a background vocal.

I understand. And congratulations. You just wrote your first chorus for a song. And you said you didn't consciously write those.

You're a good teacher. But that's not exactly, completely true.

No?

Beautiful Storm does have a chorus. So does *Dive*.

Yes. My mistake. *Beautiful Storm* does. *Dive?*

Dive is a piece that's going into my book of poems. It's for Isa. Not for us.

Laurie removes her head from its perch on her hand. She picks up the lyric sheet and sits back.

And I like the change we made in the last chorus. It's affirming. It's lovely.

If the two of you are quite done...

Devon's voice startles me. I had quite forgotten that he was in the room.

How do the two of you feel about being done? At least done with the part about writing the last song for the album?

I get up from the worktable where I've been sitting across from Laurie. I move over to where Devon is standing. I sit on the floor and I gesture for Devon to take the spot on the floor next to me—which he does.

I think we were...

I glance up over at Laurie.

...if I may speak for both of us. I think we were having

difficulty with the "we" thing. Trying to write it subjectively, I mean. I know I was. We didn't experience the breakup in the same way. We experienced it in two completely different ways. We went down two different roads. Metaphorically speaking. When the decision was made to write it objectively—he, she, they—it came quite easily after that. I suppose my initial trepidation about writing a song together with Laurie was unwarranted.

Devon puts a hand on my shoulder.

Not at all unwarranted, Isaac. You needed to establish your position on this in your head before jumping in. Ever so sorry about giving you a hard time about it at first. I do have to say…

Devon pauses as he reaches over into the cabinet for the scotch and two glasses.

…watching the two of you dealing with what you've had to has given me some exceptional insights into some of my former… relationship baggage.

Devon finishes pouring the scotch and places the bottle on the floor in front of us. He hands me one. I rise to cross over to get some ice from the freezer in the breakroom. I circle around by Laurie's chair.

There's a good side gig for us. Relationship counselors.

Laurie has been listening attentively to my conversation with Devon. She does, however, seem to have a thought of her own that is in her head and has been waiting for the appropriate time to bring into the conversation. I guess she realizes that this is the time to do so.

I'm not too sure about that relationship counselor thing. I've been thinking. Our relationship is just really weird. I'm singing songs… and I know that other bands have been through this… I'm singing songs that Isaac wrote about me…

about our relationship... about our breakup. It's all good. It's interesting. It's just... weird.

I realize that there is something I don't know about Devon that I'm now curious about.

Devon, I've never asked you this before. On the topic of relationships... is there a significant other in your life?

Yes. You've met him. Sort of. My husband, Simon. He was here for the last party. I didn't get the opportunity to actually introduce him to you.

Husband. But no ring?

We thought about it. Just never went there. I guess we figured the rings were not that important of a thing for us.

I continue into the breakroom and open the freezer. I gesture to Devon regarding any ice for his drink. He gestures back to decline the offer. Laurie points to the bottle of scotch.

If I were to accept the offer of the gig as your relationship counselor, would that entitle me to a drink as well? Isaac gets one but I don't?

Devon moves quickly to get another glass from the cabinet and pours some scotch, which he then places on the table in front of Laurie. I grab the glass and head back over to the breakroom for some ice for Laurie's glass.

Oh so sorry about that. Didn't mean to forget about you.

I understand completely. The two of you seemed like you were about to have a nice bonding moment. I didn't want to get in the way of that.

Devon and I exchange a glance and a nod. I hand Laurie's glass back to her. Devon proposes a toast.

Congratulations. Here's to being done with, at least, writing this song together. Impressive that the two of you were able to do that without... you know... Now we only need to finish up a few things musically and then we can begin recording this last one.

We clink glasses. Devon isn't finished with his thoughts, though.

I must say, I will miss having you around the studio, Isaac. Do stop by every so often. I would hope you think of us as friends.

I do. And I will still be around. Especially since my daughter and Laurie's daughter are in a relationship. This is all far from over.

Devon, I would like a few moments alone with Isaac. Would you mind...

Laurie gestures toward the door to the workroom. Devon looks at both of us. Nods. He grabs his copy of the lyric sheet and, glass in hand, he makes his exit, closing the door behind him. He glances back through the window at both of us for a moment, then moves on to the other end of the studio.

I watch as Devon moves away then look over at Laurie.

Is something wrong, Laurie?

No. Not at all. It's just that our reconnecting... our attempts to resolve our old conflicts... our trying to get our questions answered... they always seem to get interrupted. I'm just trying to...

Laurie takes another drink from her glass. She dips a finger in her glass and swirls the scotch and ice. She has that same look in her eyes that she gets when she is figuring out if she should say something or how she should say it. She tucks her hair behind her ears. I make an effort to help. I sit down at the table—next to her, rather than across from her— this is the first time I've done that.

Laurie. Seriously? At this point in our relationship? Just go ahead.

You've never asked me... directly... specifically... why I needed to end our relationship.

I know. Believe me, I know. I am very aware of that.

There is this pause. This is the most uncomfortable I have ever seen her.

Isaac, do you have a question for me?

I sit back and stare into Laurie's eyes for a moment. I then lean forward towards her.

I do not. Some things are better left undisturbed.

No need for that kind of closure?

Knowing the answer to that unasked question is not the closure. Not needing to know the answer to that unasked question... that's the closure for me.

I sit back again.

And, ultimately, it wouldn't... doesn't... change anything at all in our lives. Unless you have some insatiable need to tell me.

There is a pause. Laurie studies my face. She looks in my eyes. She tucks her hair behind her ears.

Thank you, Isaac, for treating our past relationship so respectfully.

I suppose that's the only answer either of us need.

Chapter 50
RESPECTFUL DISTANCE

I…** like to… I want to… I need to… surround myself with people… with souls that have a positive energy. With souls that pull that energy out of me. I'd like to think that that includes you in some way.

After saying this, Laurie takes a sip from her glass and seems to be waiting for my response. I consider this carefully. I glance back up at Laurie.

Are we becoming friends?

Isaac, that's not that easy of a question. It's not just the two of us. Our relationship, whatever it is, affects and includes Paul and Isabelle, and the kids.

Laurie, we already agreed that, once this album is done, you would be working on your next album. I would go back to working on my next book. We'll see what happens with the relationship that develops between our two daughters. My wife and your husband seem to be getting along extremely well. Otherwise, as far as the two of us are concerned, respectful distance.

Involved in each other's lives but aware of our boundaries?

Isa has had no problem at all with the two of us working together and being around each other to work on this album since it's not more than that. Out of respect to my marriage —to both of our marriages—spending some time together because Gen and Ro are together is fine. Doesn't anything more than that beg the question, from our spouses, why we feel the need to be in each other's lives... well... any more than that?

And if Ro and Gen's relationship blossoms more?

We adjust our boundaries. This doesn't have to be that difficult. It's not that easy—but it's not that difficult. Respectful distance.

Okay. Deal.

We make a move to clink glasses but realize that they are now empty. I make a move to retrieve the bottle from the cabinet. Laurie stops me.

Wait. I'm going to ask you a hypothetical. Purely hypothetical.

I gesture for her to continue.

What do you think would have happened if we married?

I take a deep breath. I look at Laurie. I sit down.

Considering who we both were back then, maybe we would have been... okay. Maybe we would have made it work. But, honestly, given the people we've become... well, we'd never be as happy as we are with the people we are with now. Given who we are now... ultimately, it would not have worked between us. The fact is, however, that we've become who we are now because we weren't together. There is no way to know who we'd be together. And perhaps...

Perhaps?

Perhaps you were right all those years ago. The relationship had played itself out. And it was not meant to be anything more than it was.

At this moment Devon's face appears in the window. He points to the door with a questioning look. Laurie and I look at each other and nod, acknowledging that we are done. She beckons Devon to enter. He opens the door and just leans partially in. We can hear, in the background, the music for *Ghosts in the Mist...* at least what we came up with to get us started.

I've been listening to the demo you made of the basic guitar part for the song. It does work nicely with the completed lyrics. I don't believe we would have to make many changes, if any at all. Perhaps change *can't* to *cannot* —*it's* to *it is*—*they're* to *they are*—for the tempo and phrasing. Things like that.

Devon, you can come in and sit with us. We're done with our conversation.

Not now. Thanks anyway. Just wanted to check in. It did look like you two were done. I have some thoughts I want to go write down. I have an idea. I'm hearing a violin in my head for a certain part of the song.

Devon starts to back out of the workroom and shut the door. I stop him.

Wait.

I pick up my phone.

I'm sending you the phone number of a violinist. A friend of mine. A close friend. If you do decide...

I look over at Laurie to include her in this.

...that you do want to have a violin, give her a call. Her name's Olivia. She just did some violin for a jazz album. She's good.

Splendid. Thanks.

With that, Devon is out of the doorway and back down

to the other end of the studio. I turn from watching Devon leave back to Laurie. She is smiling at me.

What are you smiling about?

You're good at this.

What is this?

Handling all the small details. You're good at the big picture stuff as well. But I've noticed how you deal with the other stuff too. Organized. Efficient. Get right to it.

Thank you. This has been interesting learning about the writing and recording part of all this after decades of enjoying just listening to music. Getting to be part of this side of it has been an education. You've been patient with me. Thank you for that as well.

Devon's face appears again in the window. He knocks on the glass. Laurie again gestures for him to come in.

You don't have to keep asking to come in.

Okay. I just had the thought that the title of the album doesn't really work anymore. We never thought about that as we started to include less of Laurie's own songs and more of Isaac's lyrics and collaboration. What about *Ghosts in the Mist?* Since that one was a true collaboration between the two of you. Well, more so than the other ones. Any thoughts?

All three of us take a moment to ponder this. Laurie speaks up first.

I don't like the idea of naming an album after one of the songs on it. It puts too much focus on that one song.

Laurie looks at me and has a pensive expression on her face. She is, indeed, deep in thought. She rises from her seat and goes for a little walk around the workroom. Devon and I watch her do this. We exchange a glance between us. After stepping back over to the table, Laurie picks up the list of the song titles for the album and contemplates the list. She looks over at me again. It's a sweet, searching stare. She looks around the workroom... again at the list... again at me. She tucks her hair behind her ear. Eventually, she offers a suggestion.

In These Little Moments.

I smile at this.

I like that... a lot.

Devon nods his head and responds.

That's good. It works nicely.

The wide grin on Laurie's face tells me that she agrees.

Well, there it is. The new title of the... our album. Devon, you go do your thing.

Devon starts to move back into the studio.

Good. I should be able to finish the rest of what we need to up quickly so we can begin recording *Ghosts in the Mist* in a few days. We'll get a release date set. And then our launch party celebration. And, hey, congratulations again on completing that song and the album. That's pretty cool.

As Devon closes the door behind him, Laurie sits again.

Speaking of celebrating... it would be nice to get together again with you and Isabelle and the kids. Our house this time. Sam is now back here, isn't he?

Yes, he is. Just. That would be nice. Isa and I have a dinner with friends scheduled the day after tomorrow. We can plan something for us two or three days after that. If that's okay.

That's good. Natalia isn't back from her trip yet. She will be, likely, in time to be at our launch party.

Laurie moves the list of song titles closer to her and grabs a pen. I see that she is writing *Ghosts in the Mist* as the last track title. She then writes the album title, *In These Little Moments,* at the top. She looks up at me. There's a tenderness in her eyes that I have not seen for a very long time.

Second chances in life are nice, aren't they?

I would say so. They don't come our way very often. I have very few regrets in my life... but a missed opportunity is a sad thing.

Laurie smiles and nods.

Chapter 51
THIS DINNER PARTY

Our laughter has just abated a bit. We've been taking selfies, adding some bizarre captions, and sending them out to all of our kids. That wasn't exactly what was so funny, though. The responses we were getting from our kids was.

Dinner has long since been finished. The table has been cleared. Dishes have been placed in the dishwasher. Em and Matt, since they hosted, are still in the kitchen fidgeting with some stuff. Several of us have offered to help with the last of the cleaning up. We've been admonished and sent off to the living room.

The evening is winding down. Ric and Gabriel have already said their farewells, are gathering their things, and heading toward the door. Keli and Gene are about to do the same. Olivia and Akiva are sitting next to us in the living room.

Okay, everyone. We'll see you next time. Akiva, give me a call about that thing we discussed.

Gabriel calls this out to us as they are about to leave. Akiva responds that he will. Keli and Gene, close behind them, wave at us as they exit with the other two. We hear some cabinets and drawers being closed in the kitchen. Em and Matt, having finished up in the kitchen, join us, taking seats in various places around the room. Olivia takes out her phone and shows it to me.

Isaac, I got a phone message today from Laurie.

From Laurie? Not Devon?

Who's Devon?

One hand is holding a wine glass. My other is wrapped around Isa's hand. I place the glass on a coaster and reach over to take Olivia's phone and look at it. I see Laurie's phone number.

Devon is the producer and recording engineer for the album. He has this idea about adding a violin part to this last song. I gave him your number.

That's what the message says. I didn't answer it since I didn't recognize the number. She says she googled some of the albums I've played on and likes what she heard. She asked if I would come to the studio soon to play what they have in mind. Do you mind if I do?

It was my idea. Not the violin part. That was Devon's idea. But when he brought it up, I suggested you and gave him your number... I didn't give your number to Laurie.

I hand the phone back to Olivia and pick up my glass again.

That would be splendid... to have you play the violin part.

Can you describe it to me... tell me what it's supposed to sound like?

I don't actually know. The lyrics were written. Then we had a melody for it. Devon said he had an idea for a violin for a part of the song. But I don't know what he has in mind. But do go to the studio and have that conversation with him.

I will. When is the next time you are going to be there?

Right now I'm not needed for anything specific. I'm on call if they need me to okay a change to something. The others are doing the stuff they do to make the song into a recording. I would be happy to go over there with you, though.

That would be nice. We don't get the chance often to do something together. Just you and me. And we could have lunch together.

I know just the place for lunch. It's not too far from the studio.

Isa, who has been listening to this entire exchange and nodding her enthusiasm for Olivia doing this, chimes in.

You could introduce her to Tonya. She was our waitress when we were there. She's fun.

Olivia looks over at Isa.

Would you be joining us, Isabelle?

I would love that.

Isa then turns to me.

Might this be happening on a non-workday for me? Like a Saturday or Sunday?

They have opened up the studio for a work session on a weekend if it is more convenient to schedule things that way. Like the day we met at the studio and all went out to lunch. I think this depends on when Olivia and Devon agree to meet.

But Laurie was the one who called me.

Yeah. Interesting. Do respond to her. I'm curious why the call came from her and not Devon. Would you like me to handle setting this up for you?

No. Thanks for the offer. I can respond to Laurie. I'll call her back tomorrow and schedule it. I'll let you know when I'm going and we'll meet there. Akiva and Isabelle can come along if they're able to. If not, it'll be just us.

How nice. And if you like what they have in mind and you decide to play it... we'll have even more fun at the album and book launch party... which everyone is invited to. Matt, since you're in the music producing business as well, perhaps there are some connections to be made there. I would think, after this idea for the violin part is taken care of, the album would be completed and ready to go.

I realize what time it is. I finish the wine in my glass and rise.

Thank you, Em and Matt, for hosting a lovely evening and the lovely wine. I believe my exotic wife and I...

I hold out my hand to take Isa's.

...should be heading home.

Isa rises and puts her hand in mine. Olivia and Akiva also rise and prepare to exit.

Oooh. Exotic. That's a new one. You continue to surprise me.

Chapter 52
THAT DINNER PARTY

The music playing is a piano piece from a favorite new age album. There is something about that piece of music that feels like my college town. There's no obvious connection and I wasn't really listening to a lot of his music while I was in college. But it does have a certain feel to it. Almost—but not quite—a synesthesia thing. I hear that piece of music and scents and images come back to me.

...but I am curious why the call to Olivia came from you and not Devon.

Laurie and Paul's house is an older house with a charming style. Most of the décor revolves around music and Laurie's instruments. Ro is with us... as are Gen and Sam. Just like our earlier gathering. Well, not exactly like our earlier gathering. We were all being a little more cautious around each other then.

There is an air of welcoming and warmth. It's partially the house. But it is also the vibrations of the relationships. I glance over at the younger generation. They are sitting out on the patio. The ladies, arms intertwined, are paying close attention to some exciting story that Sam is sharing. I over-hear a few comments. Something about his being able to usher at the Oscar ceremony when he was living in Los Angeles. I look over at Isa and Paul. They are in his den engaged in an intense discussion about interior design and looking over copies of the magazine for which he is the art director. There is giggling from both groups... well, I would have to describe it as giggling from Sam, Gen, and Ro and outright laughing from Isa and Paul.

I'm sorry. I missed what you asked me.

Laurie turns her attention away from her husband having a conversation with my wife. She looks at me.

I was also distracted by watching what was going on with our kids and our spouses.

Your husband and my wife have connected in an interesting way.

They have a shared interest. Paul is very passionate about what he does. He's passionate about many things. Especially me.

I offer a sincere thought.

I am happy... very happy... that things seem to have worked out nicely for you.

Life has its... suffering. But I like where I ended up. You seem... at peace... happy, yes... but more at peace.

Life has its suffering. I, too, like where I ended up. With whom I ended up.

Laurie changes the subject.

You asked me a question.

The phone call to Olivia. Why did it come from you and not Devon?

I wanted to connect with her personally since we were interested in possibly having her work on the album. It all worked out rather nicely. We liked the way she played and

Devon recorded her playing the violin part. Done. The only thing remaining is a little bit of mixing and the album is completed.

But that very first phone call to me came from Devon and not you.

Laurie pauses for a moment. She looks down at the floor. Then over at our kids on the patio. Then over at our spouses in the den. Then, finally, back up at me.

I didn't know how you would react if the call came from me. I was scared.

And now?

Laurie smiles at this and simply shakes her head. She beckons me to help clean up the remains of dinner from the table. She grabs the serving tray with the food I brought.

This was good. What did you call it?

Chicken Chasseur, but I used just a little bit of white wine and I used a bit of marsala cooking wine.

Nice.

You have no idea what the difference in taste would be, do you?

I know I don't care much for white wine.

We both make our way into the kitchen with the items from the table that we've gathered. Laurie places my serving tray on the kitchen table and covers the leftovers with foil. I cross over to the sink and set the dishes that I have in my hands in it. I begin to give them a quick rinse before placing them in the dishwasher. Laurie moves over to the sink, turns the faucet off, and leans back against the counter.

The dishes can wait until later. I do have to admit... there is more to the whole me wanting to make the call to Olivia thing.

Really? And what is that?

I have to admit, I was curious. She is a friend of yours. I wanted a little peek into your life.

And?

Olivia is lovely. I like her. And her violin playing is wonderful. It added just the right texture to the song. I love how it just floats in the background.

Paul calls out to us through the opening between the kitchen and dining room. Isa is a few steps ahead of him.

We're heading out to the patio. Come join us.

We do so. The sun is just starting to set. There is still a dim glow in the sky. I settle into a spot next to Isa and Laurie sits down next to Paul. A slight breeze flows across the patio. The elders of the group share stories of things from the past. A chance to fill in some details of scattered moments of our lives that led us from there to here.

The younger of the group shares plans for the next few days as well as further on forward. Gen and Ro discuss things they intend on doing together and are using words such as *eventually* and phrases such as *when we get around to it*. There is a distinct sense of comfort between them. It's nice that they do include Sam in some of their plans. Sam and Gen have always been close. It seems that Gen, too, appreciates his companionship.

Sam asks about the album and book launch party which is now being planned. He has a friend, Bhavini, someone he has been dating quite a bit, who will be flying in from California to visit. She wants to see his new apartment... and him. He would like to bring her along. She's a lovely young lady who we've already spent time with. We would like to see her again. We all agree that he should bring her to the launch party.

By this time the last of the light has disappeared.

Candles and a fire pit are lit. The couples slide closer to each other as the thickness of the evening engulfs us.

245

Chapter 53
FADE TO BLACK

Thank you, Derek.

Our gathering has been a fun and enjoyable afternoon. The gathering for the launch party for family, friends, and studio crew is a large one. The first celebration was a smaller group, and the workroom at the studio, although a little bit crowded, was fine. Devon, along with his husband, Simon, has offered us the use of his house for our album and book launch party. Most of us gather in the rather large main living room. Some are congregating in the kitchen. Others are in the den or out in their backyard.

A slight breeze causes all the curtains in the room to billow. A cat, perched up high on top of a bookcase, looks down upon us curiously.

For what, exactly?

My gaze goes from Derek to Amelia standing beside him. I catch a glimpse of Isa, Laurie, and Paul in the middle of the room deep in conversation. From the way they are looking around the room and gesturing to a variety of things, it looks very much like they are discussing some interior design stuff. At the moment they are focused on several lovely pieces of art hanging on the walls. I guess Devon and Simon are very financially comfortable and they do have exquisite taste in décor.

Making this all happen. I don't feel, necessarily, as though there was something missing from my life had it not happened, but all of this is a nice addition to things.

I glance back over at Isa and the others. I see that our own circle of friends, Olivia, Akiva, and the others, have joined them in their discussion of the house. After a quick look around for Sam and Gen, I see them coming in from the backyard with Ro and Sam's girlfriend, Bhavini. Natalia, Laurie and Paul's youngest, is also with them. She had, as Laurie had said, returned from her trip in Europe in time for this party. She is a lovely young lady. And it isn't just due to the fact that Sam is involved with Bhavini now. Regardless, Sam and Natalia would not have liked each other the way we were joking about that one afternoon together. They all just seem to be getting along well and enjoying each other's company.

I turn my attention back to Derek.

So, again, thank you. Working on the album has been a groovy experience and having the book of poems and lyrics published is a wonderful thing, as well.

I'm glad it all worked out so nicely. And everything between you and Laurie?

Looking back over at Isa and the others, I see that the younger generation has joined the elder group in their conversation.

Going well. Gen and Ro have settled into a good relationship. Isa and I are pleased that they have found each other. Isa and Paul have found some common interests and are getting along nicely.

Well, that's all good. But I asked about you and Laurie.

I shift my eyes back to Derek and smile.

Went from awkward... to strange... to... to nice. We're fine.

Amelia has a question for me.

Will you be working on her next album with her?

This doesn't seem to be a straightforward, simple curiosity question. There is a tone to Amelia's voice and an expression on her face that leads me to believe she's asking about something more.

I don't think that's going to happen. This has been a lovely and interesting experience. It is nice to have reconnected with Laurie. I hope... I think... we've been able to embrace some important elements from our past back into both our lives. It hasn't—if this is what you are really asking—taken away all the damaged feelings from our past, but it has softened them. At least, I'm able to appreciate certain memories of our past more now than I did before. However, Laurie and I both have other projects in our lives to get back to. I did enjoy learning about songwriting. I hadn't written anything other than novels for a while. I do need to get back to working on my book. I hadn't written any poetry in many years. Maybe, if I take a break from working on my book and I write something Laurie can use, I'll send it to her.

That would be nice.

Amelia and I both smile at each other and nod our heads. I include Derek in our conversation again.

What about you, Derek? Are you going to be involved in promoting her next album?

No. For me this was a fascinating thing to do to challenge me with some creative orchestrating of events. Books and music albums are not really my thing. I just got hooked into it when I met Laurie and you at that party and the opportunity presented itself. I was interested in seeing what I could do with the songwriter and book writer connection thing. I do have a few other things that need my attention.

Isa comes up beside me and hands me a glass of wine.

You should try this.

I take a sip.

Nice. You did make note of what kind of wine this is, didn't you?

I did.

Thank you.

Isa links her arm with mine. I gesture to Amelia and Derek.

We were just chatting about our next projects. I was just about to say that it's been great meeting and working with Derek. And Amelia—we didn't really know each other very well in college—but after thirty or so years...

Getting closer to almost forty years.

True. It's been nice to see you again. First the reunion, then the gathering at the studio, and now the album and book launch.

Amelia nods.

Let's make it a point to get together once in a while. Just because the work you've been doing with Derek is done doesn't mean we shouldn't see each other more. Everyone says, all the time, "We'll get together soon," and things like that. A little time goes by... and you don't. Even more time goes by. I think we all just forget that it's worth the effort to break our routine every so often to do something worthwhile.

I agree. I had, for so very long, isolated myself from our college group. Not necessarily consciously or on purpose. It's just that life gets so involved revolving around... things. It takes effort to break that cycle. I'm guilty of it as well.

Except for Jonathan, I hadn't really made the effort to see any of you.

I glance up to see Olivia and Akiva coming through the crowd and up to us. I introduce everyone.

This is Olivia and Akiva. Akiva works with Isa, and Olivia is the violinist we brought in to play on the album. This is Amelia and Derek. Amelia is a college friend. Derek is a consultant on the album.

Hands are shaken and greetings are spoken. When Derek and Olivia shake hands, he makes a comment.

Ah, so that's your violin work on that last track. Nice touch.

Thank you. Nice meeting you. Isaac, thank you so much for bringing me in on the album and including us in this celebration. It's been lovely.

It was great having you involved.

We are going to be heading home. As are the others. We'll see you at our next dinner.

Kisses and hugs ensue. Olivia and Akiva go to meet up with the others. Isa and I wave at the rest of our group of friends as they head toward the door. I turn back to Amelia and Derek.

Excuse us for a little bit. We're going to go find our children.

I hold my hand out to take Isa's hand and escort her away.

You go ahead. I was just chatting with the children a few moments ago. I'll chat more with Amelia and Derek.

As I move off to circle around to the other side of the room where I last saw our children, Laurie and Paul emerge from the throng. They seem to be heading in the opposite direction. When Laurie sees me, however, she leans in close to Paul and says something to him. He looks up and over at me. After turning back to Laurie and nodding, he continues moving off in his original direction. Laurie comes towards me.

The launch party seems to be a pleasant success. Everyone looks like they're having a good time. Are you having a good time?

Me? Having a blast. Isa and I were just having a conversation with Amelia and Derek. Now I'm just attempting to track down our children.

Last time I saw them, they were in the den. They were admiring the collection of music albums Devon has. It was nice to meet your group of friends. They seem like a very dynamic group. The kind of people you would gravitate to. I just wanted to check in to make sure you were okay with what was going on. You did tend to be quite the introvert and big gatherings were just not your thing. Are you still that way?

I am, indeed, still very much that way.

I cast a glance around the room.

Still, I'm doing okay with all this. Thanks for being so thoughtful about it. And...

I turn my gaze back to Laurie.

...I have been wanting to say thank you for something else.

Such as?

We were kind of thrown back together.

Kind of? We were basically ambushed by a group of people at the reunion pushing us into this. I know they just thought they were being encouraging but... so, what are you thanking me for?

Seeing it through. We could have both backed out at any moment. Just given up. Or just been adamantly against this right from the very beginning. You gave it a chance. I know both of us were reluctant... cautious...

Trepidatious?

...at first. But it turned out to be a very worthwhile thing.

Yes, it did. The album is a good album.

I'm not talking about the album. Having had this experience and second chance, I think our lives make a little more sense now. So, thank you, again. And I also want to say, I'm sorry.

Sorry? For what?

For whatever. Fill in the blank. Whatever it was that... you know. The reason for the breakup. My reaction to the breakup. You have my blessing to attach that sorry to whatever you want or need to. I just don't think I ever said it and I wanted to.

Laurie looks into my eyes for a moment. She looks down for a moment. She looks back up into my eyes.

Same. Ditto. Whatever you need it for.

Laurie and I simply stand there for a moment. Understanding the full importance of this moment. We are interrupted by the gleeful arrival of our children and Bhavini.

Have you seen that record collection in the den?

The kids go on and on about the extensive and eclectic collection of LPs that they have been looking at in the den. Laurie and I are listening to our kids, enjoying their enthusiasm. Sam comments that although the collection probably has only a few more albums than my own collection, there are albums in this collection that he's only heard about from me, but never actually seen a copy of. Every so often, as the kids share their excitement, Laurie and I glance up at each other, look at our kids, and smile.

The kids' conversation has shifted to various other

things. They are making plans for a day trip all together before Bhavini has to fly back to L.A.

Isa joins us. And I see Paul coming towards us as well. Isa comes up behind me, takes the glass of wine from my hand, takes a sip, then places it back in my hand. She puts her arms around me and her head on my shoulder. Paul steps in next to his wife and takes her hand. The four of us exchange glances as we listen to the plans the kids are making.

This all does have a kind of surreal feeling of one of those moments in a film where everything has somehow all worked out and all the characters are enjoying the moment... as it fades to black.

Chapter 54
THREE YEARS LATER

There are these moments. These moments mark your life. These moments alter your course. The wind for your sails arises from an unexpected place. These moments take you on a different path. Perhaps a very different path than you ever thought you would be on. Things will never be the same. Sometimes this is in drastic, staggering ways. Sometimes this is in subtle, elusive ways. And this happens so very many times in our lives as we constantly evolve.

We have several blankets set about on the Great Lawn in Central Park. Isa and I on one. The remains of our picnic lunch on the Great Lawn have long since been cleaned up and cleared away. I have the perfect music to complement the day. I have some new age harp music playing at the moment. Over to our left are Gen and Ro with the baby girl they adopted. The last two years have been an exciting whirlwind of them moving in together... getting married... and then hearing that their adoption application was accepted.

Not just the last two years, but the last three years have

been quite... interesting is not the right word. They have been interesting, but it's more that there have been changes... growth... a slight shifting of our lives around. Almost like a rebuilding. It's not like our lives were stagnant before, but... growth... no... enlightenment... that's probably the closest I can get to our combined experiences the past few years.

Our album was successful. It received some nice attention and some nice reviews. Laurie had gone on a little mini-tour to promote it. My book of poetry did well. I stayed friends with Devon. After the tour, Laurie then went right back into the studio. Her third album was all the songs she had put aside when we started our collaboration—the songs that were originally supposed to be on that album—plus a few more she had written. I did not have anything much to do with that album. Laurie did take a poem I wrote for Isa, *Dive,* and set it to music and included it on her album, though. I went back to working on the book I had begun and was very happy with it. Now I am working on writing my next book.

Although we are now more connected due to the fact that our daughters are married, Laurie and I have settled into an amiable relationship. Isa and I do not spend much time with Laurie and Paul other than the occasional family gathering. It works for us.

It's been a lovely afternoon with a performance of *A Midsummer Night's Dream* at the Delacorte Theatre and a stroll through the Shakespeare Garden. And then later, we plan a visit to the Peculiar Pub in the Village to finish off our day together.

On the other side of Gen, Ro, and the baby, Laurie and Paul are lounging on their blanket. Their daughter, Natalia, has brought along her boyfriend. Their son, Raphael, is also visiting with his girlfriend. They, along with Sam and Bhavini, are enjoying tossing a frisbee around. Devon and Simon are also with us and are on their blanket over to the right of Isa and me. At present they are in a deep discussion regarding the merits of the actors in *A Midsummer Night's Dream.*

If we listen attentively to the wind... if we don't fight it... after a cycle of suffering and rebirth... and a touch of atonement... we end up where we belong.

I look over at Isa. I watch her watching our family. I listen to the wind.

www.ingramcontent.com/pod-product-compliance
Lightning Source LLC
Chambersburg PA
CBHW070454300726
48975CB00007B/2176